James Beard is a retired teacher and lecturer who took up fictional writing in his retirement. He is the author of two plays, one a piece of musical theatre and has previously been published (*The Why Question*. Austin Macauley Publishers, 2023).

He has stood as a local councillor and has served on a number of academic bodies and was a college governor and a trade union representative. In his free time he has involved himself in community and neighbourhood projects. He enjoys travel and gardening and family time with his family and grandchildren.

This book is dedicated to our daughter-in-law, Melody, and her wider family, a number of whom were murdered in the death camps during World War II, and for whom there will never be an adequate answer to the Biggest Questions.

James Beard

THE HOW QUESTION

AUSTIN MACAULEY PUBLISHERS®

LONDON * CAMBRIDGE * NEW YORK * SHARJAH

A CIP catalogue record for this title is available from the British Library.

ISBN 9781037103612 (Paperback)
ISBN 9781037103629 (ePub e-book)

www.austinmacauley.com

First Published 2025
Austin Macauley Publishers Ltd®
1 Canada Square
Canary Wharf
London
E14 5AA

Much of the material for the historical context of this book was gleaned from visits to the Royal Artis Zoo in Amsterdam, and the Jewish Museum in the same city.

The cover image 'Monument of red bricks' at Westerbork Camp was transcribed from the author's visit and photographic record, in February 2024. Each brick represents a Jewish victim of the nazis in Holland during WW2. The bricks are located in the former roll-call square.

For all our many friends from the Netherlands who have 'held open the curtains' for us to share, to see, to learn and help understand.

Part 1

Those who have a "why" to live, can bear with almost any "how". Victor Frankl (After Nietzsche)

'Homo homini lupus.' Latin Proverb. 'Man is as a wolf to man.'

1

Times have changed. A pregnancy outside of marriage in Holland in the 21st century is rarely a cause for concern, let alone the deep shame that drives a young woman's family to leave behind their neighbourhood and friends. And Amsterdam itself is much different now, except for its much-loved buildings and monuments that still speak to an earlier golden age. In the Plantage district itself, over here is an exquisitely restored and gleaming Hollandsche Schouwburg theatre, with its porticos and colonnades. Over there, across the busy road—even though that fragile oasis of peace for terrified children has long since gone—its neighbour, the old building from where many lucky ones were passed over the boundary walls that is now recreated as the school it once was. This place where the ghosts of heroic student rescuers still linger.

It couldn't be a more special day. A day to commemorate. For here, more than 80 years on, crowds are gathered to show their respect to the victims of war and to pay tribute, too, to the extraordinary bravery of others.

A flag is waving alongside a noisy, though largely good-natured crowd, protesting against struggles now being fought in another part of the world, and where sides must be taken, as was always thus. They are a reminder that *'the war to end all wars'* is little more than a fiction of men's colossal conceit. And here today, at the inauguration of Holland's first Holocaust Museum, yet another marker of that folly.

Alongside the grand and the good, and our country's king, come with me now, as anyone may, through the wide open doors of the Hollandsche Schouwburg, past the reception area and out into the open space to the rear. Once it echoed to theatre people, bringing into new life cold print on a page, and excited and eager audiences seeking out ever more make-believe. As some deeper truths too. But do remember, as you tread this way, some more recent times, where, behind locked and bolted theatre doors, a terrifying indoor prison and execution route for tens of thousands of innocents bound together only by the accidental burden of belief.

That tall tower of the memorial to the deported Jews is now flanked by seating for guests. Along each side wall are set newly-dotted *tears*, convex Perspex domes, each of which holds the human story in pictures and words of just one life; an infinitesimal fragment of those millions persecuted. Be wary now, for guests are moving towards their seats. The weather is kind in this open-air space, and there are TV and broadcasting cameras and a dais at the far distant wall, which is for the dignitaries. And there are also two young people who believed once they were in love, but now, quite unaware of each other's presence, taking their places. And more than five thousand kilometres away, there is a great-grandmother in Canada who loved a liberating soldier and paid a price, but then gave him the very best of her life.

Who in this place today will ever forget this children's choir, and the haunting strains of poetry set to music and transcribed from the written record of the hopes and fears of the young in yet another evil place, the transit camp sending them to certain death? Our young man, for sure, will regret not making more effort with his Dutch.

An announcement, and there comes to the dais a slight, wavy-haired elderly lady who walks unsteadily with a cane and is graciously received as she's helped to the podium. A nervous moment as they have to adjust the microphone, which has been set at a height for a king, and there is much fussing, but please, do listen to what she has come to say.

"I will speak with you today in English. First, I will welcome you and want you to know that I have had a lucky life. I'm a survivor. If you are familiar with Schoenberg's tribute to the heroes of Warsaw, you will know its refrain *I cannot remember everything* and for this, as for me also, I must apologise. For I was so very young then, but you may just have caught a glimpse of me as you passed by; my elder brothers and I, playing hopscotch in the street, just around the corner there," with a sweep of the hand "and likely not even have given it a second's thought. Just as thousands more doing what children do. And never a concern for tomorrow. Until one particularly dread day."

"How could we ever forget it? We children named it *the day of the stars*. Those horrible yellow stars. On sleeves, on blouses and jackets, on coats. And, truly, that is precisely the moment when you *did* notice us."

There is a hush in the building now, a hush more powerful than the traffic sweeping past outside the open doors. A hush so powerful that it makes tears in many.

"And afterwards, from some, for sure, a new-found respect. For the others, the star tells what they already know in their poisoned minds. And in that moment, though we did not conceive it, we had lost our mothers and fathers, our aunts and uncles, our nephews and cousins and all those who cared dearly for us, and we did not know where they had gone.

"Think it. *We did not know where they had gone.* For after all, just who was there to tell? They had disappeared in the blink of an eye. But some things a human being always remembers, and I know now, in my years, that it comes down to the kindness of others. And in this place especially, and across that road—"

She points, and just momentarily appears to lose her place, but continues on:

"Across that road began our journey into light. Across that road was more than a place of learning, more than a house for prayers, even. No. Much, much more. Rather, a community of saints. You will know the history, I'm certain, so I will simply recount our dread time of waiting."

"A time when we wanted more than anything to be with our mamas and papas, as you can imagine. But you know, when you have someone to feed you and someone to dress you and someone to warm you with cuddles, and right over that wall, a beautiful garden where the school principal would allow you to play, and a classroom too for the little ones to rest, you are dangling just that little sliver of hope. Our guardians were both Jews and non-Jews, and they taught us a single game over and over. A game of pretend; always it was pretend. Both day and night.

"Pretend you are someone different; pretend those dolls are real; pretend that wall, over which you hope to be lifted, is a mountain you learn to climb; pretend you are in a lifeboat which has set out to rescue you. And most of all, pretend to be brave.

"And though these memories are faded, I have one clear picture in my head all these years. Of a girl, not much older than some of us children, with eyes the colour of a deep and inky blue sea, like magic pools, forever dissolving and resurrecting themselves.

"Not much more…but that name still. A name I can never and will never get out of my mind. That girl whom everyone loved. A girl named Eleonore."

14

2

Eleonore's St Bernard dog (her code for a *searcher*), with its message for her friend, Freyja, that she was safe, never did arrive at its intended destination. Or if it did, Holland being at that time a dangerous and murderous place, then the message was ignored, or betrayed, or worse.

Many records from that period are sketchy at best, and yet some events are still coming to light many decades later, so everyone must be patient. The present mystery is that I am drawn to the self-same city in the Netherlands that shelters my great-grandmother's past.

You need to know that great-grandma Freyja is now what many call an *elderly lady*, a term which understandably she resents, perhaps no more so than when some hapless victim of a crime is described in terms. She beats up the TV voice so mercilessly that I have learned to tread with care.

Though I'm far away from my native Canada, here in Amsterdam, Jaap back home keeps me up to speed with what's to do across the pond. Jaap, granny's first and only Dutch child was conceived at the very end of the German occupation, and has only an old lady's fading accounts of those grim times, but it's the very best we have. His younger sister passed, as had their father many years before. So, what's clear is that we can't guarantee long lives in this family. I guess we must try hold on to our Overgrootmoeder (her Dutch title) for as long as we possibly can.

3

Spring 1942

I have given up my attempts to write my diary in code. Partly because I am feeling braver, partly because all my attempts at getting my words out sometimes come to nothing. However, mostly because my friends in the zoo say that they have safe storage for my writing.

Often, it's hard even to put pen to paper, especially now that the Nazis have come to murder Papi. That's not what they'll tell you, of course, he being given the chance to 'work away'. But anyone can see if you steal someone's work in the first place, why on earth should you want to give it back one day? And why only there, at their special camps, and never once a chance of visiting? Perhaps they imagine we're stupid? Of course, everything has been done officially, as it always is in this country. Date of the month, time, station and terminus details for departure; clothing, money and other allowances, all clearly set out.

Even a printed band to wrap around an arm.

We stand here, on the platform, silent and fearful—mumie and I, as the hundreds thronging around are marshalled by officials waving billboards with destinations posted. Even though we are promised to say our goodbyes, it's only at the very last minutes as the trains are steaming up. And why isn't there a single Nazi soldier in sight, which tells who really is behind all of this? Some relatives, having been taken in by stories of new opportunities, are treating it almost as a holiday, waving handkerchiefs and blowing kisses whilst the engine boilers first hiss and then roar to a crescendo.

I run alongside Papi's train. It's gaining speed. Faster and faster, it goes. I let his hand slip as we approach the platform's end, and with smoke streaming cruelly towards smarting eyes, this seems merely the beginning of a likely long dying.

4

"Hi Tom. It's pokey your room. No bigger than a matchbox. How do you manage?"

I am already discovering the bluntness for which the Dutch are renowned, and I reply, "And you're a prick," which is what Bart might likely expect from a North American dude. Even from a new-found Canadian buddy.

We first met on the day we signed up for our postgrad studies, and I believe I'm a genius even to have found a place in this Amsterdam of sky-high rents and too many people. It's hard by the university admin though, and the floating flower market and bookshops, and the only downside I see is mapping a path through daily hordes of tourists.

"And what if I tell you why I have a pokey room, wise guy? What about that?"

"At least you could manage to keep it clean," a double whammy this, and whilst I could likely blow him over, period; he, unlike most of Holland's unnaturally tall and fit-looking locals, is rather more than a little, shall I say, flaky around the body parts. So, I resist. I tell him that my lovely landlady is a professional woman and I get twice the price for my rent, resisting the temptation to admit that she's nothing more glamorous than a translator.

"Anyway. Bullshit aside. What do you think of the place?"

Quite unexpectedly, he grabs me and, somewhat awkwardly, kisses me three times, once on the left cheek, once on the right and then again on the left.

"Wonderfully Dutch room, Tom, tiny maybe, but perfectly formed. And that's the very last kiss you get from me, eh? Just showing you the Dutch way. Nothing more, man. So, what say we split?"

We struggle down the steep staircase, single file out of necessity, and enter an outdoor hubbub of people and cycles, a jumbling of accents, colours and scents; stirred and shaken all together as if in some giant potpourri. See here, there's fried and smoked fish and fowl, and sweet and sour. And, over there,

17

musty and sweetly flower-smelling from the Market, and Bart says, "I insist, I buy you a gift," which I soon learn is the Dutch way for many a greeting. And so, it's to him I owe the debt of a tiny ailing pot plant which they give away for free at this time of day when all the tourists disappear and which I know I am duty-bound to leave on show until it perishes through lack of both light and water.

5

Back Home

Dear darling, Tom. You probably won't forgive me for writing so soon. I'll worry myself to death until I hear back that you are settled for sure. I have promised your folks that I will keep them updated, and I will have Jaap check that I am not getting stuff wrong or making silly mistakes, as you are bound to do at my age.

When he said that you were living near the flower market, I had to admit a little flutter of the heart. I still keep a vivid memory of a day when Eleonore and I, her papa and my uncle, all met there and we drank double lemonades for good measure, and rode our bikes like flying dervishes and hoped against hope that the moment would never ever disappear.

It was one of those rare, hot, airless days in Amsterdam when time never ends. You'll remember Eleonore, Tom? But perhaps here's not the best place to hog the story of me and my best ever friend, because you will make your friends quickly too, I'm sure.

One thing about Amsterdammers is that they take you at face value and don't have too many prejudices, except maybe about spending too much money. (One trick is to go to the markets at the end of the day. Did I tell you that before you left?)

So, hey, everything back here is fine with us Canucks and all send their love and maybe will get over to see you before you end your studies. Except that this old horse is maybe too old for that now?

Once I know everything is okay with you, I will write you and share some secrets of the times, like why I never forgave my parents and relatives or even Holland, for what happened back then. However, isn't that some of what you're studying right now? So, guess there's an even chance you might make it all hook up one day.

But really, Tom, just get on with your life and have plenty of fun, which is what I think is right for you right now. I know my own studying was a struggle, what with a small child and little money and all. But I so loved all the finding out about things I didn't ever know before, that it never bothered me too much. Those answers to the *why* questions. So, au revoir for now.

With all my love. PS: Enclosed 50 dollars. Don't spend it on stamps or the phone. You hear?

Your Oma.

6

Early Summer 1942

There were no more tears after that day. What can prepare or even comfort you in the pain of that deep void, now just an empty space, once so filled with life? Nothing can ever be like it was before, nor ever again I fear.

No cheery familiar greeting, small kisses on the cheeks. No dressed table and the morning eggs nestling in their bowls; it was always the morning eggs, and wafts of freshly brewed coffee, and enquiries as to how the night was? No, not any more of this, in spite of mumie's efforts to make up for everything.

For sure, she knows how to keep me busy though, and it's my grown-up job now to rummage amongst the chickens for those few precious speckled jewels, because even our animals are half-starved. And after a heavy wind, to search out fallen chestnuts for drying and grinding, though the bread still turns out hard and gritty, however hard you try.

Few dare even mention papi's name for fear of bringing down extra sadness. The embarrassment on neighbours' faces when they ask, 'How is he, and is there any contact?' And a sudden jolt when everyday pieces of his former life: his watchcases, springs, tools and winders, scattered around and unloved, are briefly glimpsed, as if urging him to return, and those busy fingers, the wide grin of pleasure on his face for work well done, take fuller form.

Always, though. Inside and seeming forever and ever; this dull and cruel ache.

7

SS and Police leader Hanns Albin Rauter sits upfront these days in his armoured chauffeur-driven official car; no longer fearful about the possibility of surprise assassination.

For, of course, the enemy is now few in number and all too well-known to Hanns. Moreover, in these days, they are effectively neutralised by the thousands of state and Dutch police as well as his own soldiers.

Little local difficulties can always be snuffed out by the agitators in the National Socialist Dutch Workers Party, firebrands all and entirely reliable. When he truly reflects upon it—not a trait running deeply in his nature after all, for he is a man of action, a man of the hour—this whole nation is unashamedly on the winner's side.

The Daimler is, at this very moment, pulling away from Adama Van Scheltemaplein, where the headquarters of Zentralstelle fur Judische Auswanderung is located. Hans has assured himself that his colleague, Herr Funten, has all the necessary resources to ensure the compliance of dissenters, be they communists or Jews. The fact that compliance might well embrace various forms of electrical and surgical hardware in order to enable the speedy gathering of intelligence hardly concerns Hanns. He has recently joked that efficiencies necessary for the war on the Eastern front may require a return to the old-fashioned water and bath treatment! After all, there's water in abundance in this country, isn't there.

But no. His deputy has a fine track record, and affairs are safe in his hands and so he gives it little thought. The same cannot be said for his Jews, however. Indeed, he spends many valuable minutes each day thinking about them.

Remarkable, isn't it, that they have invented two of the world's major religions, including the one where you are beseeched to turn the other cheek? He wouldn't be at all surprised to discover that they had something of a hand in the third. But they are slippery characters nevertheless. They run their own affairs well, as befits crooks centuries steeped in their book-keeping and usury, but they are equally masters at the art of black-marketing.

The chauffeur is headed out for the Eastern Docks, where Hanns plans to keep a surreptitious eye on the Amsterdam Police Battalion, Sybren Tulp, which helps transport those taken in the roundups to the trains headed out to Westerbork. For he's not altogether a trusting commander, as he is aware that even hardened and ruthless operators aren't necessarily immune to the pretty face or the twirl of the skirt. Or more likely, the clink of gold coin or diamond.

8

The Amsterdam thing has been drip-fed into my life from an early age. It's crazy, dude. After all, we didn't see anything of her past, but, from great-grandmother still:

"Don't ever forget your Dutch half, Tom" as if that should be any more elemental to me than that my great-grandfather's forbears had been Irish. Signs her correspondence, *Oma*. Always. In her head, she's just Dutch Grandma and just another of those quirky aspects of her life that, to my knowledge, excepting a single visit to the Netherlands years ago, there's not been a single connection with her country of birth.

Few photographs, letters, or any old ephemera to be seen, nothing except her first child's native Dutch name. But everyone-yes everyone, has heard this one single thing—her Eleonore story. If they really were the very best of friends, why was there nothing further after the war? My sister and I used to puzzle over it, maybe we asked once or twice. Perhaps, as for many survivors of that period, it was all too painful. Or her memories were too blurred or distorted. In any case, who really knows?

Much more to the point, what the hell am I doing here ruminating, whilst stretching the whole Dutch thread to three generations? I won't even begin to burden you with my scribblings in the university library, but just to revisit grandmother's time, and even beyond, and the darkest of days at that, may, well, set you to wondering, eh? I'm not a psychiatrist, but feel free to take some kind of stab at it. That likely sets off another *why*, and then yet another.

9

One evening, on a trip out to the students union bar with friend Bart, I met *THE GIRL*.

She, apparently out of nowhere, said, "I just love your accent, it's cool."

And me, "I'm not Dutch."

And she added, "And I'm not Saint Nicholas."

So what is it with this? I'm clearly not to be flattered by this total stranger, but hey, she's a beaut, nonetheless. Maybe in her spell already?

Me; "Are you studying here?"

Bart speaks across to her in their native language. No way I can deal with that and they fall into a shared joke. Jeez. I'm all the more unsettled.

Bart; "Try asking her name. You never know, you might make progress."

She, before I could utter a word,

"If I tell you mine, then you can tell me yours."

She's the driver here, for sure, and I'm stuck for progress until I get *Irene*. She is, at present, studying 'the mathematical properties of chance and luck'. And yes, she's clearly on a piss-taking riff, and so, for calm;

"Jeez, interesting. You know, I have a cousin named Irene."

"And I have a relative by name Black Pete."

Now she's clearly taking liberties with this hoser when I'm merely blown sideways as she takes my hands in hers, fixes my gaze with her darker-than-hazel eyes, and asks, "So then, whatever your name. Weren't you just lucky to have met me tonight?"

I'm not sure I can frame even a single syllable in way of reply.

10

April 1942

The zoo is my salvation, for here, in the midst of war and occupation, is a green oasis of calm and life, and my free entry pass is my lifeline. Sheer luck sometimes counts in this life they say, and having a best friend whose mother is the director's friend! How can you better that?

Sometimes, I come to Artis with mumie or the cousins, more often than not alone, for my mother needs the whole day just to keep our heads above water. Shopping needs to be planned for, because those with J passports can only visit at fixed times. And naturally, by that time, so little remains. I see from the look on the faces of the good Dutch people that they have us in their hearts. But aren't they as much trapped in this nightmare as we are?

It's a still chilly day here, as the winter celebrations fade in memory. The trees which launch the native herons and perch the chimps are rapidly returning their colour and their life.

"Eleonore, my dear," a voice that first startles and then warms as Gert comes into view, wheelbarrow and rake in attendance. "Just where have you been hiding all this while? Are you avoiding us?" A skip of the heart. Do I tell him about papi? Do I pretend that things are all fine? But he has already sensed my hesitation.

"We've really missed you, Eleonore. All of us. Come."

I follow him around the familiar hay lofts, past the rocky goat prominences, and the new vulture enclosure with their sad, silent sentinels on their long poles. He tells how things are different now, what with the feed shortages, and the culling of some animals because of the lack of workers. Mostly, the young amongst them who have been reassigned to more necessary work. And yet the Nazis say they adore animals. If they won't keep our animals well, just how less likely are they to protect us? We share Gert's liquorish drops.

"How is moeder, the cousins," and then dread, "and Freyja?"

The very mention of her name stops dead the moment and, whilst at first the question hangs, it grows heavy as I struggle for some kind of reply. Is it the nightmare of papi that has quite locked my dearest friend away? And now here's Gert, rendering her real again. And at this very moment, that's the only thing I have a desperate need to know. Where is Freyja now? Is she happy? Is she searching for me? And, hope upon hope, does she still think of me as I do of her?

And I can't hold in the tears, even as close as Gert holds me, for he doesn't understand he should never have asked, because, yes, these are two nightmares now to haunt me. And I glimpse the giant vulture's wings unfolding like great painted bats, held open in supplication as their incessant screeching begins.

11

University of Amsterdam

Hi, Jaap. Hope you're keeping an eye on the old lady? Her letter enclosing dollars came in handy, eh? But serious stuff first. I have to tell you that I've got some luck studying here; not just my Dutch friend, but a rather sweet translator landlady who has offered to help with some of the more difficult source material for my studies. Whilst there's heaps of stuff on fascism before the war, you need to know I'm heavily focused on my one particular angle; on what I tag the 'theatre of fascism'. You get? The symbols and staging and representations and all that jazz, requiring the digging out of contemporaneous newsreels, newspapers and magazines, banners and posters. So, of course, my landlady Hanny comes in way more than handy. And she's cool!

A question, Jaap? Just take yourself back a few steps. What in hell was all the stuff with flags, uniforms, leader worship, martial music and parades? And its links with death and destruction cults? Just how come crazy? Whatever. Anyways; heavy stuff aside, back to real business, which I just can't let go.

My buddy Bart, my trusty guide to the delights of the city, and Irene (don't ask, we'll see), joined me in celebrating at an Indonesian place. It was a rice table, of course—they say rijsttafel here, which the entire population greedily wolfs down. Get to tell Oma if you will, I have a hunch that this is the colonies' revenge for the Dutch occupation! Anyway, picture the place.

Dead in the centre of town and amongst its garish lighting and the swish of cars and whistle of cycles, there's hardly space to squeeze onto the lumpy banquets stacked against walls with their painted murals of Jakarta or Malang or wherever. The air sweeping in through the carved portals is heavy with this coffee-like ciggie aroma, and I'm trying my very best to keep Bart out of Irene's eyeline. (That's jokes to you, Jaap, thinking he even has a chance!) Anyway, I'm picking my way through the fish wrapped all about with banana leaves, topped with crunchy fried onions, stuffed aubergines, spices and whole boiled eggs with also, much use of the napkin, and Bart's pestering and stabbing bits from my plate, only then to announce, *let's share,* when the door swings and in comes this guy and parks himself right next to Irene.

Not difficult to miss him, jeez no, for he's into the *leather and chains* look. So, I focus on Irene instead, fixating on a delicious point just above those lips yet to be chanced. Except that my gaze won't stay fixed, returning unerringly, over and over again, to the guy's hands and wrists; distinctively decorated all over with the tiny imprints of swastikas.

12

It's hard to say what appeals most about my new buddy Bart. His research, naturally enough, though we are on quite different tracks. He's a deal way back in time, teasing out the medieval stirrings of antisemitic rhetoric and iconography. I joke that he won't discover a single survivor in this kaleidoscopic city to help dig out the truth of it all! For myself, I've posted a classified in a periodical that gives overmuch space to present-day *rightists* in the hope that maybe I might get a bite from a still-living member of the NSB, the once-main Dutch fascist party. They will be, at best, mere youngsters in that time, and near enough chasing a hundred years by now, with muddied memories or, who knows? Maybe even repented of their sins!

But as for Bart. Take music. On that score, the two of us can agree. Or not, as the case may be. Like, when did the Dutch last claim a world No. 1 hit? In his defence, Bart points to the unmatched language skills of its people, meaning we can get anyone else's No. 1's. But hang there for a moment, for here's arriving his unique take on 'Lady Madonna' and in that first listening, that singular alchemy of rhythm, lyric and melody, melds into the universal ear, so now we truly are soul mates. Not that he can hold a tune! Not for a damn second.

So I tell him we get why every other Dutch person speaks English more or less fluently, because why else would anyone—even the most desperate—try getting their tongues around this impossible gobbledygook? And so he insists that's likely also a Dutch word, and so many Dutch words are English words too he claims.

"You Canucks had to learn English, yes? How come so many dudes everywhere filch the Dutch words they really like, and then ditch all the messy ones they can manage without, and then not even the humblest in way of thanks?" (him)

And so, it raps, and you have some take on why we are true buddies. For my part, I've stretched his education with the odd French Canadian expression; he gets 'beaut' because that's what Irene is, and he's a 'hoser', a foolish person, because that's what he damn well is, anyways. But also-respect-a 'keener', because he works so bloody hard. And now he *met-ens* whenever he agrees with something or other a Canuck like me says.

Twice, he has rescued me from certain death as speeding bikes jump lights and their riders fail to discover their bells. Do they even have bells, these guys? Anyway. I forgive all, Dutch-wise, as Bart might be useful as regards this certain Irene, who I know now is Irene Fischer, and I mockingly ask, "Is she really not German, because that rings much more likely a German name?" To reference Germans, even with this Dutch generation, sparks something residual in the DNA.

13

That meal. We *went Dutch* in the end, even though my Tom (can I call him that?) wanted to treat us with his Canadian dollars. But I'd learned a little more about his elderly relative and her Amsterdam days. And he's funny too. He told me that his Oma has *made him Dutch,* which I consider more than a stretch. And I tell him back that because my English teacher hailed from the States, I have this lift at the end of each and every phrase. So, I tell him that I'm part North American.

I'm not so sure whether for the sparring or my looks that really grabs him, but that he fancies me, I do know. Because at the end of the meal, his friend, Bart, comes up with some lame excuse about having to catch a cash machine, and he'll have to dash, and can he trust Tom to see me home? Big mistake. But I'm jumping ahead already.

I have a sort of thought-out plan to walk him alongside some of the grand merchant houses peering over our canals. So, we'll do a kind of winding, twisty way back. And for no more than the heritage naturally!

By now it's getting late, and the crowds are thinning. As we walk on, the luminous lights of the centre are dimmed to little more than dull reflections on cobbles, reflecting back the night sky. We have lots to tell each other, but try as I might, I just can't shut him up. He seems bursting to shrink the whole story of his life into this single journey and without pause for interruption. Though I have my canal-side histories ready for him, what else to stem the flow, unless "I want you to know I'm not German, Tom. Bart told me you thought I might be German."

He hesitates, gives it thinking time. And then a little bit more.

"Hey. He's a buddy Rene…I didn't…It's just the name. Lots of guys back home have it too, and…Just fun, you know."

Sensing he suspects he has crossed me somehow, I grab him by the hand.

"I'm teasing Tom, you idiot. You really don't know the eternal story here in the Netherlands already? The Germans and our bicycles?"

He looks directly at me. So clearly not, I guess.

"They stole them at the end of the occupation, and we only ask for them back."

He's mid-step, but pauses, seeming unsure as to what to believe, and then moves around to face me. For one moment… and then, he buries me in a giant bearhug and whispers, "And then we brave Montreal soldiers arrived and booted those nasty Nazis away, right back to where they came from."

I kiss him, and "Thank you, brave soldier, for rescuing me."

We kiss some more before we walk for a time in silence.

"The story is just a little bit more complicated, though. Back after the First World War ended, the Germans were left penniless, so we bought up their entire bike production. That probably got right up their noses."

14

An easily recognisable car pulls into the shadow of a dockside wall, and its occupant orders his chauffeur to kill the motor. Hanns sits and watches for a while before carefully turning the handle to wind down the window. It is a scorching summer day, and he is glad to be out of the office.

For a brief moment, he reflects whether this is all beneath the dignity of a man whose greater mission is to rid this country of its entire Jewish population. But please understand what a complicated business this whole enterprise is. 'Just move the packages from A to B'. Yet for that, he needs his deputies to calculate numbers, his pro-German and Dutch police to organise the razzias, make the arrests, the Dutch SS to gather the malingerers and all of the rest.

Granted, Jews must all carry identification, but this is heavy on manpower. *Packages* must be transported, household effects to be recorded and removed, and the trams and trains to be co-ordinated also. So, it goes on. It all brings Hanns out in a sweat, and, as an exceptionally tall man, he feels the need now to stretch his legs and wipe his brow.

He steps outside at exactly the moment his attention is caught by the arrival of a fleet of dusty-grey tarpaulin-covered, open-backed lorries. There are many tens of them, he calculates, as they slow and come to rest, stirring up clouds of dust as they manoeuvre.

The Ordnungspoliziei he recognises, and notes that no one steps up to help assist the men and women contained there; largely young and middle-aged, many smartly dressed, fashionable even. A woman with braided hair, another Hollywood-style, one with a cinched waist jacket, quite unlike the usual tropes of the ugly stereotyping of his propaganda masters.

He's pleased to see his police battalion members in their severe light-buttoned tunics, standing aside to keep order. He also spots an expositor from the Jewish Council, which is as it should be. These people should help write their own fate, as they have dictated others. And no children, which pleases him the more.

For there are some things which still severely pain him. He isn't heartless, after all. He turns back to the car, to the chauffeur who is asking, would he enjoy a smoke, and he opens the clip on his silver case, takes out a cigarette, cups his hand and leans into the open window.

As the flame spurts, he hears, as if in passing, "Just like lambs to the slaughter."

It's like an electric shock.

"Out," he screams. "Schnell. Hands on the car."

The chauffeur is terrified, rushing to oblige. There are long moments. The chauffeur adjusts his legs. Hanns Rauter can't quite find the words.

"So, immediately on our return, you will now hand in your keys to security and your driving documents and your uniform. Understand? Your weapon, too."

For there is another thing that Herr Rauter cannot abide or tolerate. In his head, this whole story ends right here. At this exact point, close to the trains. Never to contemplate for a second what lies beyond. Nor can he begin to imagine for a single moment that, one day, he might be the very man who will lose much more than his keys, his driving documents and his uniform.

15

June 1942

A world without men is a strange place to live. I write 'without men', but now we have only our very young and our very old. Yet that world doesn't apply, it seems, to those who have chosen the wrong side.

It's almost as if someone, somewhere, is holding up the grand plan like a Torah scroll and is unravelling the manuscript a turn at a time, whilst most can't even begin to see the beginning of the direction of travel. If you were once a Dutch civil servant, you are, of course, now merely a Jewish civil servant; still administrating, supervising, registering, and insuring for sure. But for your own people only, none of which helps one jot those now far-fewer printers, bakers, drivers, carters, menders, and makers get work.

And now, yes, of course, you may still continue writing for your Jewish newspaper, but which these days prints only what it is told, as we all know. Whilst, at the very same time, holding out the megaphone to scream at us all about those things we are no longer allowed to do. No more owning a vehicle or driving, nor taking trams, to ride cycles, to watch films, not to teach, lecture or practise law or medicine, nor socialise with non-Jews, or even marry the one you love!

They even kindly let us manufacture our own Star of David and then demand that we must buy and wear it, branded as if cattle. Even to collect for our own charity shops, the demand that we must 'donate' to our men sent away, just like papi.

Maybe this is all a very clever Nazi trick, so that, one day, ordinary Dutch people can say they never saw any of it happen? But now, for the first time in my life, I also understand that all this points to the might of the weapons that they have and we do not. Weapons, that, at their imagining, could anyone seriously believe could hold a whole universe of people in chains? And yesterday they took down the fence that surrounds us. And straight after that, up go the signs everywhere spelling out 'Jewish District' in large capitals.

So, what is that all about? Are they playing with our minds? If only Freyja were here now. I would ask her to put on that Sherlock Holmes hat.

16

The noise and crowds are long left behind, except the whoosh of vehicles as they sweep by. Tom and I are in our own universe until one comes to a halt, or rather, it seems to skew over from the road onto the sidewalk at an angle to us. It's a bicycle and a yell in Dutch, which I've learned best ignored if slurred and angry. I feel into my coat pocket, a first instinct. *Something sharp*, moeder always warned, to clutch in your hand.

This crazy person is screaming now, quite out of it, and Tom, trying to be reasonable to calm him down.

"Hey dude. Leave it. I don't speak Dutch."

I am searching for my flat keys, pulling him away from the crazy man and closer to the steps fronting the merchant houses, looking for any possible escape.

"Forget it, Tom, just come away," I say, tugging his sleeve urgently, but the drunk or stoned lunatic confronts us now, head on, blocking our path.

"Money, you bastards," he yells. "You have money."

He is lurching forwards at pace now, quite out of control and no; no way out, attempting to slow us with the front wheel of the bike, and I can't see if he has any kind of weapon. My heart is beating furiously when a voice comes out of nowhere, in a language I know.

"Just keep walking right ahead, guys. Ignore him."

The ranting doesn't stop.

"Towards the trams," the voice says, and I know now not to panic.

I sense whoever must be bunching him in, and I tug once more at Tom's arm, and there's shouting, and a firm voice above the ruckus.

"The tram just ahead. Walk fast. Get straight on. Both of you."

In my relief, it doesn't occur to me to wonder in which direction it's headed, but we know we must. As we climb towards the gaping gap, there's a hand from behind, holding firm onto the door wrap, a hand decorated with swastika symbols, and I don't even have time to thank him before the tram doors glide shut.

17

My best great-grandson! (Tom)

Hi from your Oma, and greetings from freezing Canada. It's below zero here, so I'm thinking maybe AMS is cold too. I want you to spend some of these dollars (enclosed) on thermals and insulated socks because I remember you always said you get cold feet. And then complained you had the same gift every Christmas!

Jaap reminded me that I should tell of some of my memories of Amsterdam in winter, and yes, it often felt every bit as cold as here, though it didn't last nearly so long.

Mostly, on the holy days, we would visit a little church outside of the city, which had a frozen river nearby, always, seemingly, shimmering like a string of diamonds in the half-light. And there was a real donkey and a goat in a mock stable nearby.

Then, once inside, everyone was lit and warmed by candles, and not able to shrug off their heavy coats and scarves for fear of an early death. And always singing the same familiar JS Bach, and frozen breath rising like cigar smoke.

I remember, as if still today, those same breaths often beery, and afterwards…Hey. I'm rambling, Tom. I know. But the past rears up before an old lady and helps soothe away the present.

So what's new with you, tell me? A little bird has whispered the name 'Irene' and maybe love? So, before I hear back, you need just a little more of the person I adored more than anyone or anything in the whole world all of those years ago. No—not a mother or father, as everyone must, but a little girl with deep blue eyes, who, just like me, was trying to make sense of a great big universe out there.

Hang in there, Tom, for yes, you know something about her, but this is as much about this old lady now, and her feelings. One thing I never said enough was that for a long time, I felt that I'd betrayed her. Not by anything I did (there were plenty then who took the Judas silver), but because I could have done so much more.

That day, after the school assembly, when all the Jewish children disappeared, I made a vow. A fateful vow. Never again would I even so much as think of her. Not a mind picture, not for a single moment. Nowadays, I guess you'd say it is a way of keeping safe, protecting yourself from loss and grief. And, believe me, Tom, there are still lots and lots like this who have to keep their war *safe* inside their heads.

And after that, I'd feel doubly guilty when my parents did their very best to try to help, by suggesting this or that, and even enquiring as to my feelings, I would literally scream them out. And as you know, Tom, I can be a very determined lady if I choose to be! And much later, when my parents—

But enough, I won't go there right now. Just remember this advice: try always to stay true to whoever you love, however hard it might be.

(Three days later)

So sorry, Tom. I had to take a break, and my remembering back isn't always for the best. I just get too emotional. Let's get to happier things now.

We had a family get-together for my 90th! Yes, it's true. Can you believe, 90 years? Not everyone could travel because of the storms, but three of your great aunts and uncles were there, and your sister. They had rigged up a TV monitor, and we had lots of clips of the days when my lovely husband and his troops came to rescue us from the Dutch winter of hunger and almost starving to death. Much newsreel to see today, of course, even though I didn't know it was so severe then for myself. And they also said that the very first winter hunger drop was flown by a Canadian pilot! That I did not know.

And then Jaap's childhood in Montreal (we had a b/w recorder by then) and lots else, and as much of my long life as they thought might please me. I was even persuaded, crazy me, to bring out my graduation gown once more; not such a swell idea after the years but it brought us to laughter when I tried it on, and I remembered just how proud I was at that particular moment. Especially that I had learned to answer some of the important questions why.

And now I'm proud of you too, Tom, that you are continuing in that tradition. Tears now! Sorry, but that's me.

Please keep writing me about what you are up to (though not everything, for I was young once too) and about your friends and how the city is, and why not parcel me some of those sharp liquorish drops that are never as good anywhere in the world as in Holland?

PS: They say there are a lot more flavours now.

With all my love,

Oma.

18

I have to admit. I was sh!@ scared. I know the deal here; these things happen, just do as asked. But I'm with the girl of my dreams and how to be brave? Events seem to paralyse me. I sense Irene going for her pocket, and this lunatic is clearly out of his head or whatever.

You'd make towards people, sure, but there's no one around, only this aloneness, and everything appears constricted between me, the bike and him. And it's the guy who has to be brave, right? And then, this gift from nowhere. Total strangers who protect us, and a freak who, Irene reminds me later, wears the insignia of the Nazis around his neck and on his wrists.

But I'm really knocked back for a while afterwards, because Holland is likely another Canada, isn't it? That's how I see it. Free thinking, liberal and peopled by those just like me. And, for a while, this scary guy has got my goat and sent my confidence reeling.

What's with this brotherhood of man and all? What's with life a little less certain and the streets not such a cool place to be? If I'm totally honest, the whole thing has *shrunk* me just a little, but maybe an insight gained. It's this crowd thing. Sure, it helps keep you safe, you're protected, now more than a merc nano-particle in an atom. But think on. Might it not also make for a much *bigger* you? Like nudge your identity or your sense of yourself? After all, the very early Dutch fascists showed little, if any taste, for blaming minorities for their woes, unlike their German counterparts. But hey dudes, what the hell now? Only the other day I'm hearing 'Holland for the Dutch', so where's this story going?

And another mystery. Whilst there's all that theatre in fascism for sure, the costumes, flags, the din, and that swastika and the wolf-hook of the WA and all, back to that guy rescuing us. Complicated or what? I guess it all needs to stick there in my thesis one day, but hey, just lighten up. Who doesn't want to check out how my Irene story goes? Even I'd like to know more on that score myself! And I need to check back whether I have any replies to my classified ad.

19

I believe the loyal soldier requires much more than his German marks and his insignia. Swearing allegiance to the leader is merely a precondition. What needs to follow is a concern for the warriors' welfare, and for their emotional life too, as unpleasant things have to be done from necessity. And of course it is for the best that these things are never consigned to paper. So today is such a day for my most senior men in the SS headquarters.

We have a zoo here in Amsterdam, which is quite extraordinary, and from the very beginning, a public institution. So it is still, and must remain as such, in this new German empire. And it must be much visited, for nothing is sustained by wishful thinking.

Of course, we Germans are at the forefront of animal conservation, but for scientific enquiry, they made an extraordinarily early start here. One example will suffice. In addition to live animals, they also held a collection of dead objects, from which anatomical and other insights might be gained, and you must credit them with that and more. Of course, over time, the Jewish tentacles became stronger, and we saw sculpture and paintings of a less comprehensible nature more and more often displayed. Exotica and fantastically sentimentalised and other such, quite against the spirit of the age. Everything over-stated and over-romanticised, no less.

But then again, understand that I have my own friendly zoo director now. I don't doubt for one minute that he is a solid man and that we both reap the benefits. Indeed, remarkable, isn't it, that his own son eagerly complied with the request to help the work effort back in the fatherland? No quibbles. Helping pursue our war on communism and other such evils. And I have my eye on Polak, the Artis entomologist. When all this is over, I will retire to the Greater Empire and utilise all the new knowledge that agriculture brings to the land. That day when fertilisers are in short supply, I will look to the insect world to rejuvenate the soil. And when I can get away, I will remind myself of these days long past in visiting the universally acclaimed Museum of the Jewish People with its objects and artefacts of a deceased race, which are, at this very moment, being documented. But I get ahead of myself.

20

Montreal

Hey, Tom. Just a brief letter from your great-uncle's snowy home. I'm wondering back here, why I don't work at getting more out of all this modern tech and stuff. But then again, maybe you don't have the spare dollars to access it at your end. Anyways, any suggestions, please wing my way.

Great to know you have two important people in your life, the tattooed creature, and Irene, who, I guess, is an alabaster princess? Tell me more; I'm waiting. This is to head up that no real worries yet about Oma Freyja, but she's beginning to show the odd crack. Very positive still, when was she not? But on occasion, these days, she begins to muddle past and present, and even generations. Like she speaks of holding your late aunt's hand downtown when what she really means is her grandchild's. Mind, there are far too many grandchildren these days, even for this old guy to keep track!

Not to overburden you, buddy, she still lives independently, but you're no longer just around the corner, and, guess we all should be thinking of what the future might bring. So just let me know if she starts spreading the 1000-dollar bills rather than 100s!

Trust you're getting answers to all your history puzzles, Tom. That's the beauty of my field, eh? With engineering, you just sense problems might well end up with some kind of solutions. Even if they turn out not to in the end!

Best. Jaap.

PS: Was this worth the price of a mailing? What would a text cost me?

21

Autumn 1942

My dearest Freyja.

I have had you in my head these last few days, and I thought I would tell you just what I have been up to. I have asked Gert if he can try get this your way.

I still believe that one day we will be together again and share all these long-hidden scribblings, and we will laugh and laze around, and talk and talk and talk, as once upon a time we just couldn't stop.

When we were finally prevented from attending the Montessori school, the Jewish Council opened up our own place in the Staatsliedenbuurt. Can you imagine it? Somewhere so far away from most of our homes, with trams and bicycles denied us? Lunatic, I know. The head, Mr Goubitz is very kind and we, older children, helped with whatever we could. But when you can never be sure that the same children will be there two days running, and others never returning at all…You try hard not to imagine where they've gone to (but wouldn't that be impossible for you and your vivid imagination?).

Anyway, eventually, there weren't enough children for even one class, so I was redundant! Crazy that you can be out of a job even before you begin your very first grown-up one! But don't despair. Our council has set up an after-school youth care which is not just for neglected children anymore, and I like to choose the ones who find it hard to learn, unlike you and me. We are so lucky, aren't we?

The main thing is helping them read, but we also do craft, music and dancing and even sport. However, we are reduced to just skipping on the spot and table tennis, as space is hard to come by. There's little time for boys, in case you ask, and anyway, there are busy days for me now, as I need to spend daytime helping mumie (as still no word of father).

I'd like to have something new to wear and feel pretty in, but it's impossible now. Do you remember that dress you liked from my birthday, the velvet one?

47

Well, it's worn almost every single day, and the material is fraying. My only very new thing is my Jewish star, which even children have to wear now. Isn't that what grown-ups call irony?

And I finally threw away that doll I brought to yours, which you thought was strange at the time, but when I was so nervous, it was my only comfort blanket. I'm not sure anything can bring me comfort right now.

But I know you won't worry about me if I tell you that I'm readying my new year's resolution; from here on I will forget all the 'why' questions and now it will only be the 'how'. How to survive? How to be happy still? Because I know for certain that this all has to end someday. And anyway, I haven't lost you, have I?

I still hold you dear in my heart.
Your ever faithful Eleonore.

22

We mainly *laser* about *this, that and the other,* Bart and me. Yes, he's quick on picking up the French Canadian, even if I'm once tagged 'the British branch' (says grandma, who, after all, is Dutch and because the British stole it from the French!) One for shifting her ground, that girl, eh? Apart from the chat, he's keen to learn much more about *ma blonde.*

Not that I'm not gonna give much away, even if there was anything major to give away. In any event, tiring of evasion, we switch to our *can't think of much else to do* mode.

He: "Famous Canadian singers?"

Me: "Too easy."

He: "*The* most famous Canadian singer then. Without Googling."

Me: "Even easier."

This is what two over-educated men do to pass the time of day when not over-educating.

He: "Name just one, clever arse."

Me: "Leonard Cohen."

He: "Okay then. The *least* well-known Canadian singer?"

Now, he's playing shit. To tell the truth, it's lyrics I'm cooler at, which means I go down a treat at karaoke parties, but relegated to sketchy on all the rest of the business.

He: "Give you a chance. Within the last 50 years."

Me: "You're taking the piss. Here. Pass me another beer."

He: "So, what say you strike one up for me?"

Me: "Let's toss for it."

He pours. Froth spills over the rim and drips onto the carpet. A habit he isn't able to entirely rid himself of, judging by the state of the place. A sleety wind outside stretches a branch which beats furiously back and forth on the window pane.

Him: "Right, camarad. Your turn."

Me: "Same rules? No Googling?"

Him: "Same rules."

Me: "Any famous Dutch singer you've ever heard of?"

Hilarious giggling. All our contests end up exactly this same way. Failure to reach a final resolution. All beautifully Dutch, I guess.

23

I have to make the best of my opportunities here. I'm a lucky researcher, for I have a native speaker to aid my project, and she can focus on digging out archived documents and so forth. Sometimes, I can even persuade my landlady to accompany me to the university and those places where there are no modern digitised facilities.

But for eye-witness accounts, there are few direct translations, and Hanny is excellent for this, and for diaries and pamphlets and posters and other hard-located items. Between us, we 'parcel up' the prewar fascist movements in Holland; all quite different, yet as one in their hatred of threats from both liberal democracy and Marxist socialism. And there are many more strands than you would ever guess.

The National Socialists, of course, are well-known from Dutch history, and their oft-quoted leader's 'Whoever does not belong amongst our people must go.' And then, for emphasis, 'From the Chinese to the Jews'. Then there's the murkier WA fascist paramilitaries, whose wolf-hook symbol adapts the swastika, falsely claiming its origins in ancient Germanic tribes. Yes, and even a women's only party, the National Socialist Women's Organisation, which predictably urges women to raise a strong and racially pure nation.

No surprise that, except for the first, they were all eventually dissolved on the orders of the Germans. All too disorderly for the Teutonic mind.

She's a good friend to everyone is Hanny and I, in turn, lend a hand with her young son's homework and hide my curiosity when he reveals the marriage went *pear-shaped* (his English is excellent), so I keep well away from Irene talk or romance or such stuff as might bother him. She's of my parents' generation, so no bar to conversation there and also, like most of the Dutch, rather proud of Holland's record during WW2, which I trust won't be too much dented by our research enquiries. What we both find puzzling, however, is this recent explosion in tracing just singular family stories. But hey, whatever rocks your boat. In any event, it always feels as if time is pressing (grants run out after all), and on balance, I'm up for the view that it's the wider lens that more likely helps unpicks the secrets of the past. And there's always the possibility: what if really bad stuff turns up? What then with your family history vibe?

I'm distracted from my musings by an unplanned arrival. Irene has a library ticket too, but this is a first, and maybe not entirely coincidental.

"You know the guy with the tattoo?" she says, quite without introduction. "Well, I saw him here yesterday."

Unfazed, but curious as to what might come next, I ask, "And?"

"And," she said, "I thanked him."

"Well, next time you see him, thank him from me too. He's a great dude."

I thought that might be that, but then she adds, "Jos is doing a Masters in Social Work."

"That's terrific," I mutter, but at the same time, where am I with this, my sometimes seeming to have arrived from a different planet?

She senses my confusion. "Is that a problem?"

Of course not, and sure, I admit to not always seeing the best in folks. Yes, of course, she's right that people aren't always what they seem (or seem what they're not). Even while seeming all around us, history might be in the process of repeating itself. And here I am fooling around in the last century's horror show. And yes, I admit it, I'm real damn confused. And just how come she remembers this tattoo guy is called Jos?

"Hey. Let's go take a coffee," I say, deflecting.

24

Picture Dutch canals and their spiders' web of bridges, and dank dripping tunnels beneath, and silent motor boats with their sometimes raucous guests and their guides. And no, we kid not; though we are in Amsterdam and yes on the water, we are no way, certainly not remotely even, tourists.

Don't insult us. We are a superior intellectual species, reclining au bateau with our Grolsch (for the manliest) and champagne (where are the ladies?) And so, we are merely the takers-in of the sights. Whilst musing, obviously. As always.

"Can you get this 'where do I come from thing', Bart? You know. Ancestry and all that? I was knocking it around with Hanny the other day."

I kinda could bet on his particular take on this even before he replies, as he hasn't so far even hinted as to the existence of parents of his very own. Push on all the same anyway.

"But perhaps if there's something quite—" I struggle for the right construct. "You know, way back. Wouldn't you want to know?"

Long silence. "Quite what the hell are you blathering about, Tom? And much more to the point, why? You didn't really say it out loud."

And there it is, his irritating habit of not answering my queries by posing queries of his own. Which he knows winds me up. I try another tack.

"Let's just go with this, then. Someone close in the family, not so way back, has been responsible for some real shit. Wouldn't you want to know?"

With hindsight, I should have judged the guy better than to pose such a question in this city, once recently occupied by its enemies.

His answer "And what did your grandmother's folks do, Tom? In that same war, I mean. The one you're forever talking about."

"Great-grandmother, Bart. Great-grandmother."

But any passion in this is fast draining away, the guy is way ahead of my game. And now, I catch mention of the Walloon Orphanage as we pass by, and marvel again at this history of Holland as a place of refuge, not only for Jews but Protestant Huguenots and countless others, I guess.

We'd set out on the Prinsengracht Canal, I remember, headed for the *oldest cafe in Amsterdam* and the *narrowest house* and the *most famous church*, and *the brewery*. And so on and so on the guy is instructing us, but so deeply are we clinging to our tourist-scepticism and diversions into ancestry and some such that not so much as a single dime has stuck home.

But now we see many others of this city's university buildings, as we slip into the Nieuwe Prinsengracht, and chances are—it being that time in winter when the light begins to fade—little likelihood of seeing much more on this trip.

They fire up the lanterns on deck.

"Don't imagine I'm supersensitive, Tom, but you'll need to dig a great deal deeper than that."

What the hell is it with this guy? Still up for the challenge. Before I can frame even the stirring of a reply, he says, "Why not face it? You Canucks had it damn easy, didn't you? One binary choice. That's all you were about."

I'm puzzled by his remark. "So, help me out here, dude, won't you?"

"Then I'll make it simple Tom. Here's the deal. Volunteer to fight. Or not. Hero on the one side, neutral on the other. I'll be generous. Coward possibly. That's how it was for you, wasn't it?"

It's maybe the first time I've heard real passion in his voice.

"Life here wasn't nearly so easy. We're occupied. Likely to become a German satellite. The Allies are bombing German cities, and sometimes our homes too, on the journey home. Nothing deliberate. A mistake. But people die. Informers everywhere and easy money. Locked in. Borders closed. So small, nowhere easy to hide. So, what to do?"

His voice is raised now.

"You do nothing, or take up arms, passively resist, or side with the Germans. Or die whilst deciding. Not so easy, eh? Not so binary."

A few others now on the boat are now hooked into our conversation, and there's no real issue here, is there? He's damn right. A ripple even of silent applause around the equation. And because I judge Bart to be one of the good guys—basically solid on stuff that really matters—our generally flippant attitude takes a back seat here. What better to demand of a real friend?

But at this moment, I'm distracted by a vivid, bright glow, high up and through the tree line.

"What the hell's that, buddy? There, over there. To your right."

We are fast approaching its source, the guy is gunning the engine, and the glow takes clearer form. Fuzzy contours are now appearing more starkly drawn, super candle lit; unquestionably the outlines of dogs or wolves. And then it hits. Why ever not? We must be close by the zoo after all, and those images, and now I see more, which, with the movement of the boat, give an appearance of furtive skulking in the undergrowth, each so beautifully lit. So much larger than life.

And I'm here with Freyja and Eleonore long long ago in all their excitement and puzzlement as they imagine people hidden inside a wolf's lair or inside a monkey house. And as we sweep around the canal bend, there, high in the attic space of the adjoining building and silhouetted bright against the sky, an image of huddled refugee figures.

A Fascist Theatrical

Timeline: broken/hopeless

Cast: megalomaniacs/useful idiots/dupes

Chorus: mobs/assemblies/masses

Sets: epic (Greece/Egypt/Rome); symbols (sharp-edged/multifaceted); colours (red/black/gold)

Staging: lighting
              torchlight/candlelight/spotlight/searchlight/fire
              choreography
              monumental/
              sound
              loudspeakers/
              drums/bugles//martial
              crunching/breaking (of doors, of heads, of bones, and glass)

Props: uniforms/military/medals/insignia

Plot: singular/ insistent/repetitive/triumphal

And is that screaming I hear? Too, too loud. All too loud and becoming louder, and leaking blood from off the stage. And is it only a dream, or maybe more? A foreboding of future nightmares? And for me anyway, this research is doing me no damn good.

25

I put on the best possible show when Herr Rauter pays us what he calls *a special visit*. (I do not flatter him by using his designated SS title.) So, we were especially busy buffing up the 'Forbidden for Jews' signs, and afterwards loosening the bolts so they slew sideways out of disrespect for their instigators.

Our reception party always awaits at the gates; Herr Director, the other directors, and a number of my most-trusted non-Jewish members of the Board. Infrequent though these visits are, the Nazi invariably arrives in a shiny limousine with its fluttering swastika pennants as if to mark some special relationship between the occupier and a once proudly-designated royal institution. Today, there are other high-ranking officers in a vehicle following immediately behind. The German soldiers at the entrance point make a great show of saluting and stamping of boots, and Rauter leads his party through. The usual shaking of hands and a stiff bow from him.

"Delighted to see you once more, Herr Rauter. We are truly spoiled by the weather today."

"And to you too, Herr Sunier. You probably had it all arranged in advance, as is your way."

Much time on introductions to his acolytes. No matter. They do not count, and this gives me manoeuvring time. Today, only this one man in Amsterdam is my present concern.

"So, what do you have in readiness for us?" his gaze seeming to sweep the immediate landscape for any shred or indication of deception or intrigue. But Herr Rauter is a man who also believes in getting down to business from the off, and so it is for me to dictate.

"I suggest we walk the perimeter fencing, perhaps? You had some concerns on your previous visit, you may recall." Herr Rautner is a man who also only thinks in straight lines. And so his concerns lie solely in the safety of the civilian population in the event of dangerous animals getting out. Not for one moment does he entertain the possibility of humans getting in.

"And how are we doing in way of provisions, Herr Sunier?" he enquires as a lorry almost overtopping with bales of hay revs frantically nearby, emitting large clouds of black smoke as it does so, drowning out any chance of conversation. This is one way amongst many my colleagues fight back against the Nazis.

"It's the meat quota, unfortunately, Herr Rauter. We have many carnivores here, you understand. Depending on their rates of growth, on new additions, these things are devilishly hard to estimate."

He knows this already, nodding his assent, except that he doesn't quite understand. My calculations need to take account of the additional daily disappearance of large units of bone and gristle and more. These are easily filched after the last sheen of daylight and the final exiting of the meat trucks. A lifeline for people sufficiently desperate to take their chance. And further aided by the weakened links in the fence.

The elephants are doing their tricks nearby with the now-deposited hay bales, batting and rolling away like true professionals when the new ruler quite unexpectedly makes a detour towards the inner aspects of the zoo.

"You know, one day, I plan to make my own exhibits, Herr Director? Did I tell you that?" He has spoken before of his dreams; of retiring to a farm in the east after the *present emergency,* as he has it, and now dangles his plans to go further.

"It's the future that I'm most concerned about, Herr Sunier. On a crowded planet, just how will we feed ourselves? Like yourself, I am of a scientific bent, you understand. So marine farms for fish, pens and aviaries for fowl, exhibits to entertain."

We are diverting towards the aquarium now, and I swiftly excuse myself and despatch a messenger to summon our resident supervisor, who will answer any queries.

It is so solid with visitors on our arrival that the German guards swiftly move to order everyone out whilst we two make ourselves a business-like space in the bureau and his entourage is invited to wander the exhibits. He takes out his schnapps flask with its double spout and, with exaggerated diplomacy, asks if I might join him.

"You see how the people just love these particular projects, Herr Sunier. The charm and the practical in close combination. Quite a feat."

I forbear to point out that, of all our exhibits, the aquarium, just as the bird house and the reptile house, is the most popular for one reason alone; that it is expressly heated for the survival of its captives. Safer by far to encourage his belief in the superiority of the Aryan mind than to remind him of the human requirement for warmth. Now that we are alone, however, I must be alert to his wider intentions.

"Any improvement in the health of the wolves, Herr Sunier?" he asks.

On his previous visit, and as we approached the wolves' enclosure, he came perilously close to our residents' sleeping quarters, a place of refuge for 'our guests'. We managed to sedate an animal in good time, placing it close by the fencing, and offering up the fiction of a spreading infection severely dangerous to humans. Fortunately, the fiction appeared to hold.

26

University of Amsterdam.

Hi, Jaap. Sorry to have the news about grandma. She's no spring chicken after all. My buddy Bart has similar sentiments for his 'grey hairs', as he endearingly insults them. And yes, I guess I can imagine the sheer frustration when the moment can't be got out there, and the maddening merging of past and present in her brain. Medics will tell us where we're at with solutions Jaap, but don't we always crack stuff in the long term?

So, what's with this Canuk back here. I hear you ask? My research is progressing, sure, but sometimes I wonder exactly what business I'm into. Some days, history's like being stuck with the obituaries column and never the real exciting stuff on the front page. And hey, I don't much like the look of some of the political goings-on around this place. No longer cool I say. It's kinda like the opening salvoes in an altogether-new war; fewer bullets obviously, but still hatreds and divisions, hyperbole and slogans and epithets instead of straight talk and resolutions. All steadfastly playing out to the same old tunes. And all this in a country once thought the most forward-looking in Europe!

The one and only distraction seeing me through all this, however, is my 'love coach', whose only fault is distracting me well away from my studies! What can I tell you about Rene, Jaap; you this guy with two marriages to his scalp an 'all? But as for Irene, 'J'aime le way qua hang' as we Montrealers riff, and that's the very best I can offer. Then again who knows? Something really different around this time? I'm for sure not so stuck in a place that I'm teetering on eggshells, her being around, checking in the mirror, checking out what she's at. And the weirdest stuff of all. I even get what I don't much like about her. Crazy or what? But not a great bunch there to confess. So yeah, it's that good normal feeling of being relaxed and being yourself. At home.

On another tack, just in case you're wondering, the swastika man hasn't reared his ugly head for days now (except he's not even ugly, geez, and that's a bastard). And now I hear that he's offloaded the clutter around his neck, so he's a little more straightforward guy than before. And truly he slightly messes with my thesis, 'cos it's clearly not only fascists with their theatre and such.

Now listen up, Jaap. On the Oma front, I may get to squeeze a few days back home for a layover if I get more of this study business out of the way. Good to clear the air anyway. And am getting weird premonitions. Just give me your take. Crazy that I worry more about her than my own folks. They'll go on forever, of course. And you too Jaap, eh? Anyways, just help keep eyes on the ball, will you, dude?

PS: Enclosed a pic of Irene. One day you'll stumble across this thing called a mobile, and then you'll be with us all in the real world! You know. WhatsApp, messaging and all. Far speedier.

Always Tom.

27

Tom wants to meet up at the zoo. But not until this afternoon. So, what's with his mornings? Clearly, a romantic though, if he's an animal lover. The zoo! Anyway, I promise myself not even a mention of Jos, or tattoos or social work, because one look at that expression at the university told me everything you need to know.

He's had girls before, sure. He's dishy, why not, but he tells me nothing serious so far, and how do you read between the lines with that? It's always between the lines with Tom.

So here we are, I've clamped my bike to the railings just along the road from the Plantage Restaurant, and he's already late, and it's a freezing wind on this corner of intersecting roads and just where the hell is he now?

Until that ping, and a text: "Change of plan."

Irritated now,

"So get your f…skates on." Which works well for Canadians too obviously, and in turn,

"By the new memorial, Rene," which is as unhelpful as it gets and doesn't raise my belief in him one jot.

"Which memorial, Tom?"

"You know, on TV some while back. We watched it."

And yuk, he's infuriately vague, and so it goes until mention of the king, a wall of bricks and Amsterdam's Jews in WW2 and why didn't he start with that?

It's pretty much right around the corner from here, though, and *Be there* is all he'll get from me, but then loads of kisses back, which says he's feeling bad for stringing this along.

28

He's kneeling beside the wall on the roadside, lost amongst the countless names inscribed; one death, one murder for each brick.

"What's the family name?" he asks as I arrive. I'm puzzled.

"You know. Oma's friend. Back in the day."

And why the hell does he think I should know? I offer him some breathing space.

"Aren't you pleased to see me?"

That said, it still takes an age too long to sink in.

"Gee, of course. Sorry, Rene. Thrilled. Just thrilled," he says, struggling to his feet.

"Oh. Do come here. You damn well know I am."

"As if," I riff, and so he takes hold of both coat lapels and I get his customary bear hug.

"Still in Canada?"

Silence.

"In Canada. Bear hug," I say.

"Ah, bear hug," he mimics and, yes, this is a guy who truly needs work.

"Anyway," he says, offering an air kiss, and bursting to get it all out, "I've been feeling a whole heap guilty lately…and something the other day, by the zoo, with Bart. What do you think? Shouldn't I be doing more around this grandma thing?"

"Grandma thing?"

It's not getting any warmer in this wintry city, and this is way too much.

"The building over by the zoo, Tom. They do a great coffee there, and you can cool down and explain."

"Am cool," he says.

"So perhaps you can give me a proper welcome on the way?"

29

September 1943

It's another zoo day, *and those rare moments when I can picture nothing of consequence has ever changed, and to stroll freely without fear. There are still queues before the green and yellow entrance portal.*

Artis is one of the few places that the Nazis have left alone and not restricted or closed down and there is much of the usual excitement and babble from visitors. But not anymore the friendly smile as I hand over my pass.

"You must come inside, please, miss."

Just the tone of that voice alone makes my heart jump. I always keep an ear and eye open for the Boots, but the yelps, barks, squeals and the zoo hubbub make that doubly difficult today. And how can you have any plan anyway in this time when every plan is useless or thwarted?

My first instinct is to run, but that's an instant giveaway for people drilled in suspicion.

"Please, just come around."

At first, I hold back, but then I know for certain that there's no retreating behind the one-way turnstile. Someone inside is telephoning, and it's all a slow-motion dream, and please wait, in orderly tones, with none of the pleasantries of the past.

I'm close to danger, I'm certain, my limbs closing down, arms and legs feeling tired, my mind sluggish. I try to slow my breathing, which mumie has schooled me in, and I panic that it is all happening far too fast. The seconds are an eternity, and the queue is impatient.

"You are required to report to the director's office, Miss Grossman," and because it is no longer Eleanor, at this moment I must pray for a small miracle.

We walk the familiar path in silence, my escort and I, for what is there to say, for my brain and my speech no longer connect. And as my captor steers me towards the final turn, I catch a glimpse at the director's entrance… not now my friendly Dutch policeman stationed there, nor even a uniformed NSB, but an armed Nazi soldier!

I try to hold on to my dread, for hasn't Mr Sunier always told me never to lose trust. And yet at this moment, I have lost hope, and now it's too late. We are past the sentry and up the staircase, my legs dragging more and more, and I am feeling terrified as to what will lie behind that door.

A secretary appears, and I hear, "Thank you, Margot." And I half-glimpse a figure through the lightened room. And, as if it were any other day, I am back once more in the director's familiar office. Idiotically, I notice only one thing, that he has snipped off some of his large walrus moustache, and in this moment of madness imagine a grown-up joke that he is trying to copy Hitler's. But he comes around his desk and holds me so tight as a parent would, and he says, "I'm sorry, we have to make it so formal, Eleanor, but you know we mustn't take risks now."

The director calls for the chocolate drink he knows is my favourite of all. And he guides me to a sofa and draws up a chair, and sits alongside.

"I think we should let you get your courage back, dear girl."

We sit in silence for an eternity, and then he says, "I am wondering, Eleonore, do you remember what I told you when you first came to see me alone?"

He sips his coffee with his little finger extended sideways, which is a habit of his, and I couldn't admit I'd let him down by forgetting every single detail, but I remembered that it had been talk of danger.

"Well, now that time has come, and you must be brave and listen very, very carefully to what I have to say. Am I quite clear?"

Whatever it is, Mr Sunier couldn't be a truer friend, and he will never let me down, I'm certain.

"You know, of course, that I must be in regular contact with the Germans regarding our work: how we requisition goods and keep our accounting records and so forth? And I should emphasise that they go out of their way never ever to reveal their larger intentions."

"But you know me well, and 'keeping my nose to the ground' is my special talent. In the last days, I've become especially alarmed at the much greater numbers of soldiers visiting here. Yesterday, the largest number ever. That's a problem for me; one because they don't pay for the entrance fee. And two…"

"But more, much more for you Eleonore, an even bigger problem."

I try mumie's trick.

"I called in their commandant finally. He sat just where you are seated now, and he explained that it was necessary, all these soldiers were very necessary."

"Necessary?" I'm puzzled.

"Necessary, Eleonore." His exact words.

"You know how we're always honest with each other? Well, I shall tell you strictly," he said. "We're here to clean up your city."

I listen in silence.

"We both know what that means, mine liefste. And there's more. When I pressed him again on the matter of payment, his response was, 'It won't be a problem for you after tomorrow, dear superintendent. Just hold your fire.'"

Nothing needs spelling out now. It's as clear as crystal from a good man who cares not just for his animal kingdom but for everyone and everything else in the world too. He senses my fear and, try though I might, just how do you hold in your feelings? He places his hands gently onto my head.

"I know, I know. Come now, Eleonore. You will need to hold on tight. Why don't we take a walk? Whilst we all have the time." He picks up a napkin from the table and gently dabs my eyes.

As we pass the sentry, we receive a smart salute, and I wonder if the world has gone quite mad. I dare myself.

"Danke."

Mr Armand, as the sentry comes to attention, takes my arm and hurries me forward and whispers in my ear, "You're a very brave girl, Eleonore."

"Or maybe just plain crazy."

30

Is it odd that this member of the Jewish Council waits by the trains? I mean, in the matter of the taking of sides? And yes, I'm but a tiny cog in a wheel, but is this wheel going anywhere but in reverse? And then, who's driving the machine, you may ask? Not that they give you long to ponder these questions.

One, you're far too busy. And two, it's much too complicated, even for a permanently *stood-down* professional in the field like me. I watch closely as coffee and small food packages are dispensed, and everyone helps to hand another victim down, and I'm clear about one thing above anything else.

I am merely required to suppress my instincts to help; the pre-eminent duty of any human being, surely? I'm present only to ensure procedures are followed, boxes are ticked, and 'packages' are delivered safely. And do you see? If procedures are followed, who is ultimately to be blamed?

He doesn't sense that he is spotted. The man who is climbing out of the car. A vehicle such as this can only be the province of a high official of the ruling nation, and so I stay unmoving, stock still, giving him little ammunition for mischief.

We Jews in the Expositors branch must carefully balance our duties, you understand. Follow German precepts certainly, but ensure that they are always *by the book*. On other days, though, and if the situation looks safe, I may work on my own small project. Little by little, step by step.

This is the beauty of bureaucracy. An office that directs the organisation of the distribution of bread, and separately of vegetables, of meat, fish and food preparation is one also with many leaks. Leaks between the fields, as it were. And also, we know better than our occupiers where the dykes can lead. For of course, our Gentile neighbours aren't so well looked-after as the Nazis say.

It's not too far distant from the lorries exiting their cargoes to the railhead, and a cold beer or two won't come amiss for the boiler fireman who is catching a welcome cigarette. Naturally, it's become ever more vital that the cattle trucks are packed efficiently for let's be clear, the railway company charges by truck and not by occupant, and the Nazis value their moneys-worth as much as any. So, it all takes time. Counting and recounting, a German obsession.

My man's a regular, his requirements are various, and he has many good Jewish friends. However, it's proving to be a devil of a business. It's rather like extracting teeth. He wants me to know that he has a regular route for a reason. He lives in the city and his wife is unwell. So, impossible to be away for too long at a time. So how many more days more must I stick to the expected commiserations and his future plans, the weather, his children, his beers, and the rest? But that the journeys go well beyond the work camp, of that we are in absolutely no doubt. In no doubt either about the increasing headcounts by the day, and though we have enemies amongst everyone and everywhere, amongst those enemies are secreted some of our most reliable friends.

31

"Isn't it just that you're feeling guilty, Tom? She's not that well, and you're not that interested. You don't even have a name."

"Sure Rene, but who else might have any idea about it? After all, she was right here years ago. Right here in this neighbourhood."

"Not this neighbourhood, Tom, not anything like *this* neighbourhood."

We are walking in the direction of Artis Zoo, and he's become uncharacteristically silent. And I feel for him.

"Look, none of this can help, really Tom. The past is just that. And *this* neighbourhood? It's a joke. Where are the soldiers? The fortifications? Look around you. No more your grandmother's neighbourhood or her family and friends. No more than you and me standing here. Maybe making our own story."

We reach the corner of Plantage Middenlaan, and I want him to know that I, too, have some handle on the history.

"See that building Tom? Just after the corner there. Once a famous theatre, first Jewish, and it changed hands, until it kind of became Jewish once more in a truly wicked way."

"This time around it packed in the Jews like sardines because they were being shipped out to their deaths, though they didn't know it for sure at the time. And after that it's falling down. So, not this neighbourhood anymore, Tom."

"Straight up, Rene. I get it. Really. But there still must be something."

I can't stop the flow. This guy's manic. We move around the corner towards the zoo and take the crossing as a tram screeches by and a cyclist runs a red light.

"F…crazies," I remonstrate to no avail.

He grabs my hand tighter, and I soften. Okay, after all, this is for Tom, whom I'm beginning to love a little, and I guess he's asked for no more than to trace a name in a record. If one still exists.

"Nearly there," I venture, indicating a low-rise building, and Tom

"Just help me here, Rene."

I'm now almost chilled to the bone, as is frequent in this arctic city.

"Not until we smell the coffee," and we hop the steps into a glass-filled atrium. Stained glass and chandeliers—quite grand. Hardly moments before the waitress brings our order of two large slices of apple tart, topped with oodles of slagroom, and outerwear safely dispensed with, I offer him my full attention.

"Now, Tom," concentrating studiously on my handsome Canadian. But does he melt? Indeed, he does not. Just halts my flow.

"Maybe we're on a fool's errand?" he suggests, picking at the pastry. "You know what they say. Stuff about false memory syndrome and all. Covering up guilt or disappointment or whatever. Lots of that now."

Our coffees are sipped in silence. Just what can I say to cheer him?

And then he adds, "Maybe Oma's friend never really happened?"

He's suddenly deflated, his disappointment clear.

"For a kick off, you need a name, Tom. You don't even have a name. Face it."

"Eleonore's a name," he says, somewhat brusquely.

"Half a name to be precise, and then dates, and then—"

"Jeez, this tart's addictive, Rene. What do they call this cream stuff again?"

His heart really isn't in it after all, and it's an impossible task, and maybe it's time for straight talking.

"It's not a joke, Tom. Really. It's a dream, isn't it? And it's beyond a joke. For sure, Eleonore really was in this building, right here, all those years ago, buried in the records files of Jews, as it happens. Fact. And you're a Canadian in Amsterdam studying just how it got to be that the names became so dangerous when they were put in there. You know, your *why* question. Isn't that what you're working on? And maybe that's the need for focus?"

I'm not sure where exactly this might be going, but right now, a romantic is not what I need.

And then, from Tom "How's your Nazi?"

Quite out of the blue, and then he adds, "Just joking, Rene. Just joking."

No, Tom. We don't get to the zoo. Not this way.

32

I have found my informant. Or rather, he has found me. There, the address, written in a firm hand on a card pushed through the door. So, at least, he still might be mobile and, almost in the very same moment, why do I assume a *he*? Hanny will be with me and will make the arrangements.

By her account, an early card-carrying member. Joined just around the time Hitler became Chancellor in 1933. And quite male in case you wondered. Yes, quite male. She enjoys the skirmish, does our Hanny.

"A cantankerous old bugger though. Won't use the English language even if he could. Languages belong to people, he says. Ballsy, don't you think?"

Ballsy's not an everyday word for Hanny.

"Anyway, he wants it all recorded. Doesn't like the risk of being misquoted. Knows all about you guys."

"We guys?"

"Ulterior motives."

So, we settle on a written transcript from Hanny and an audio recording from me.

The Uber is Hanny's idea, as is the meeting at hers, although he has to 'be back before nighttime', which I guess means don't keep me too long. I fantasise he might want to sweep the place for bugs, so darn suspicious is he. Then again, what turns out when we meet is not quite what I might have imagined.

For starters, he appears much younger-looking than you'd expect. The same generation as great-grandma for sure. "And I still keep myself fit" after the introductions, his handshake firm still, a full head of hair, whiteish and bright blue-grey eyes.

"Erik," he offers, and then adds, "You didn't really think that I wouldn't speak English with you, surely? You're a Canadian after all."

Divide and rule? Chippy character? Too early to tell. (Note to myself: Take some time to read him.)

As Hanny makes coffee, he lowers his voice conspiratorially and says, "The young lady was quite intrigued," nodding towards the kitchen area, "about which language to use."

I'm bemused.

"Dutch makes it all the easier for her to make notes, doesn't it?" I suggest, but he won't be drawn.

I take time to place my laptop directly before him. "No tricks here, you see."

He doesn't rise to the bait. Hanny appears with the drinks.

"Sugar and milk?" she requests, somewhat brusquely.

"No sugar, bedankt. For a long time now, I learned to do without in the war."

An uncomfortable silence.

Then, looking to Hanny, he adds, like he's playing some sort of game, "So what exactly is the problem with our noble Dutch language, Frau—"

The man knows next to nothing about her, but we aren't here for the game-playing, are we, Erik, and Hanny, in reply, "Fine, sir. You choose the language, I'll decide just how I call myself."

I notice he's doing his best to glimpse my list of prompts as I make the last few tweaks to the equipment, before powering up. Seeming unfazed by Hanny's coldness, he launches straight in, in English.

"So these are amongst the reasons I joined: keeping fit and keeping Dutch. You need to hear this."

Straight in. No subtleties.

"Keeping Dutch?"

"We needed to safeguard the culture at all costs. One of our very first actions, I always remember. Not so fashionable these days. To return to the Dutch naming for the months, for instance. Less in keeping with the Latin ones."

"Listen, Mr Adams," he adds, as if suspicious already of my motives, "you don't need to bother to check the details in what I tell you; when I joined: my party card, number, where the rallies were held and so on and so on; it's long been documented."

Still to move to my check-list of questions, he seems determined to keep the floor. I interrupt him.

"How's it going, Hanny? Does he need to take it slower?"

But there's little stopping him now, and okay, no deal, she can always transcribe from the laptop later.

"Now you can get to watch the newsreels for yourself, so please, believe what I say, young man. For one, I tell you clearly. It's the idea that drove us from the very beginning, not any of the other stuff, but just the spirit it created."

"The idea?"

"When I joined, at best, it was just a neighbourhood lark, a bit of excitement. Young kids, you know. Mischief sometimes; true. But when I left, there were so many of us it was as if we were Roman legions on the march. And that's what we always set out to do. Grow the idea."

"When you left?" I query.

"Later. I tell you," he says.

He's sipping the coffee now, gazing into the middle distance, and I'm in no way sure how to plug the silence. Jeez; he's completely dictated the terms. Hanny has stayed completely silent so far, but, looking up from her transcript, she suddenly switches to Dutch.

Something she wants to say.

"All the newsreels I've seen show you're always dressed in black. Making mischief, you said. More menacing than that, don't you think? Harassing people on the streets, kicking them when down. How do you imagine that made people feel?"

But no way he's to be knocked off course.

"English, please. For your colleague. The violence? I'll say tit for tat. No more than that. Believe me, young lady, there were many different types amongst us, not just the roughnecks your propagandists write about."

"Men from the offices, the bosses, respectable types—no different from you. But put a man in uniform, and you are moulded into one. No real differences, you see. And not one of us could stomach that now we are become a mongrel nation—mongrel political parties, mongrel newspapers, mongrel…You name it. Missing the centre. No real heart."

I'm struck by this expression used over and over, the animal analogy. He's in full flow for sure.

"And marching. We marched for spectacle, to be seen. For us, a risk, I admit, but we were admired by many. Only the traitors would make trouble for us."

"Traitors?"

"The usual. Communists and anarchists. Church deniers."

And all the while I'm hearing this, I'm thinking, *This man is a surviving miracle, his body with little trace of serious ageing, clear skin, diction clear and voice strong. But it's what comes out of his mouth that seems all too polished, too knowing, and far from a muddled or hazy recall, as if everything happened only yesterday.*

"You know, they gave me that party card when I was thirteen years old. We were living in Utrecht, and I found a weekend job cleaning up after the 'Volk en Vaderland' presses closed in the middle of each night. There's oil and grease and rags and papers everywhere.

"Paper? No shortages for the party news there. And around the comings and goings of the men who delivered and sold, I could settle in to read. I learned a lot then. More than ever before or since.

"So, then, some fella had become disillusioned with it all, and they reprinted his card and number and put my photograph on and presented it to me. I felt so proud that day. When I finally left school, they gave me an apprenticeship in exactly that place.

"So perhaps no mystery, that key to the perfect recall. Daily and weekly infusions of propaganda. All of one mind. Brook no argument.

"Of course, there was little work to be had at that time, so I struck lucky. Not like in Germany, of course. Plenty there—" It was left hanging in the air for a moment. But then, "And far less trouble with their Jews."

33

Just what exactly is the protocol in this business? After all, it's now a world of researching more than ever before, a world of hard-contested subjects.

First, I have to have it straight from the guy's mouth, that's for sure, otherwise, the less authentic, even compromised the data. So, how do I stand with Erik? In this immediate moment, this here and now?

He looks straight across to Hanny at the mention of Jews, as if expecting some reaction. I see that she is somewhat unsettled, but it's my project, she knows it, and will she understand my keeping schtum? Am I complicit? I shift direction.

"You mentioned keeping fit, Erik. Remember? Keeping fit and keeping Dutch?"

He relaxes.

"Exactly right. That was a lark that was. A real lark. The boxing, weightlifting and running, and anything to build up strength. It was needed, you see."

"We Dutch were growing sloppy, and we got discipline from all this, the outdoor life and the marching with its planning and need for order. This appealed to our young minds. And don't forget, we needed protection."

"Protection?"

"From the hooligans everywhere, who didn't show respect. You understand? For our homeland, for the church, our womenfolk. And damn it, least of all, for our history. Do you know how important history is, Mr Adams?"

The irony is risible.

"Free thinkers, they called themselves, anarchists and crypto-communists to a man. Verdomme. Not history, no. Propaganda."

He's increasingly agitated, and I see his eyes moistening. Passion here. And then, "You mentioned the Jews, Erik."

It was as if he had been struck across the face with an open hand. Indignant almost.

"Please, turn off the recorder now," he orders. "And also, you," indicating Hanny, "may not write this."

"And if we don't agree?"

"Then, I walk away. Here and now. And deny everything."

Jeez, he thinks he has achieved some point of equilibrium, and that doesn't seem quite fair. He hesitates, and then Hanny leans towards the laptop and presses the *off* button. Erik appears vindicated.

"So now I start—" he begins.

"And so you may now stop, right there. And then you may leave," perfectly politely but as cold as ice.

"You've had your moment in the spotlight. You are no longer welcome in my house. Not now, not ever."

34

"It's about time you wrote her," and my conscience pricks.

We are at Bart's, surrounded by half-drained beer cans, overflowing ashtrays, and an unmade put-up corner sofa scattered with the fragile remains of our recent lives, crashed out. A real gong show. But, then again, what would life be without muddle and confusion, hangovers and reliable friends? He's also an Amsterdam local and he has wised me up on Irene's talk of Oma's friend and the zoo records, some of which were destroyed in the firebombing during World War Two.

So what the hell did I know that we were in the exact same spot of the civil registry where the city's family data had been stored, many thousands with that fatal added tag of the God they worship? And jeez. To add insult to injury, *ma blond* had just walked out on me.

Okay, to be exact, something I said that upset her. So, it's a bummer all the way. And that's not even to begin to countenance grandmother.

"So, what do you suggest I write, wise guy? An old woman who's losing her mind."

You know this; how words can sometimes just spew out, but hey, old age is an unfathomable gap, difficult to process from this side of the chasm. And the exact words I do need?

"Anything, Tom. You're reeling, but how is she to know? Just tell her anything. How will she ever know?"

Focus, focus, I urge myself; head too thick and still reeling from the extremities of the previous night. So, I work at getting some sort of grip by lamely tidying and binning odd remnants of this and that at the sink. And *inventing* stuff? This is just one tip too far.

"Look dude, it's family. Got it? How could I live with myself and anyway—" I don't have anywhere much further to go with this.

"In that case, just settle on the lovely Irene. She'll lap it up. True romance and lovey-dovey and all of that. And the zoo stuff. What about that?"

"Never got to visit the zoo," I confess, shamefaced. "Let's say distracted *én route*," in way of putting off further enquiry.

This is how guys digress in matters of the heart.

"But the wolves, you idiot. We got to see the wolves. That will take her right back. She'll love it."

"So, what say you do the damn writing, Bart? Add in whatever you like. You're for sure the best liar between us."

The predictable mock-fight that follows puts the issue quite out of mind. For now, at least. The sofa tidied, the air freshener overwhelming the brewery stink, the calm after the storm; time for reflection.

"What do you really make of it, Bart? You know. Oma's state. Maybe I should get to see her. Over there. What do you think? She could die."

"Die she will Tom; that's a given. But maybe not today. And look. If you take the girl along with you, there's no need to scribble her at all."

Take Irene? But we're not even an item. In the everyday sense of that word. Not much beyond a *Frencher* (you can guess!). But I don't tell Bart this. It would be a blow to a guy's pride.

35

I've been happiest of all in this place, I've been enlightened, excited, always enchanted, but never before this sinking feeling, a halfway house between dread and terror.

"You must not go home, Eleonore. Whatever else, you cannot go home. Listen clearly to me now." He grips my arm as we walk. "The Germans are almost certain to find your mother, but this isn't the end of hope."

He surely can't know this, but Mr Sunier is my truest person living, so I hold my breath to stop my tears, and he knows it and he squeezes my hand so hard that I sense we are in this together.

"Don't worry about what's left behind, we will come to that later. The only thing now is that you will stay here with us." It's said firmly, as if there's no arguing. "And we will find you a safe space of your own."

So many questions in my head, and I know that I must shut them out because even to question says there are other options. He's only to speak one word to the Nazi on the door, and that is that. We both know it.

We continue on past the almost-submerged zoo-man, thigh deep in his long black waders, his elongated pitchfork scooping up the debris directly beneath the chimps pirouetting on their wires, but my world feels at that moment never again to become normal.

I try my very best to be brave, but you know it's a lost battle when Mr Armand hands me his large white handkerchief. And he knows, also; best to keep me right away from the Wolfs Lair and our secret and the 'Jews are not Welcome' sign, for it is in this place here where my most hopeful and now my most cruel memories are stored, and he sees that the last thing I need now are memories.

36

Tom has asked me out on another date. I shouldn't really be ungrateful, but this far it's evident, and with the one exception of the Indonesian feast his elderly grandma paid for, we haven't even as much as *gone Dutch*. Going free is clearly his default position. But he's my guy, and he's down-to-earth and decent (his words), and this is the student life after all.

And it's King's Day here when we all take a holiday and celebrate our lovely Dutch culture where we are free to mingle and laze and to drink beer and raucous noise from whatever bands. Also, to eat oliebollen and bitterballen and poffertjes and to enjoy gezelligheid is all that should be desired in life. I remember as a young girl, when you look through all your childhood bits and pieces, and parcel out the no longer required (and never really loved?) and extras begged from parents. And you spread out your blanket on a pavement and street which you have all to yourself and maybe swap or scribble your prices on a card and then the dog bowl for strangers' cents and euros, and it's a very first for my Tom.

He's amazed at the amount of stuff that can be swung from shoulders, trundled or strapped to bikes, and inside car boots and then the courage of the kids asking a return way above value, and always the drift of brewing coffee and spent coffee grounds, sweet cinnamon and cake, and the accordion man. And so much beer at 11:30 am! But, fear not, that I do not remember.

"Hey, good to see you guys. Safe and sound, I see." It's a voice I recognise, and though Tom is headed in a different direction, I turn him right around, and steer him to this grown-up man and his grown-up stall offering all sorts and types of war memorabilia.

"Great to see you, Irene. And your buddy?"

Tom hesitates for a moment, then, perhaps thinking better of it, leans over the badges, helmets, uniform tags, the myriad medals (they can't all be authentic, can they?), holds out his hand and drawls.

"Pleased to meet you, man," in his finest Canadian, which is nothing more than to impress, and Jos

"Just trying to eke out the grant, buddy," as if to explain his present incarnation as a chronicler of war, and Tom

"I'm amazed at what people do," before softening. "When we're poor and down and out."

And then adds in, just for good measure, "Well done for you, anyway, Jos. Some sucker has to do it."

Which mightn't strike exactly the right tone, I think.

"Anyways, you guys owe me a drink, I'll be done by four."

This seems pretty non-negotiable to me, and in any case, why shouldn't my two knights go head to head in battle?

37

I have a visitor. Lovely Gert comes to see me, explaining that Mr Sunier must do his very best to keep his hands clean, but that doesn't matter because those hands will be your safe hands now. And he liked my Hitler moustache joke.

I feel happier that I didn't ask the director for help in finding my Freyja, even if he is a good friend of her mother. Who knows where that might lead to? And it seems Gert is determined to talk about anything but the present danger.

"Does moeder still bake German bread?" he enquires and what about my cousins, and how is my teaching coming on? And never once a mention of father or Freyja. And with his chat—along the way, he has taught me lots of life lessons about the sensible things to think, and what best not to, which is a true gift from grown-ups. And he has also brought supper, those meatballs and Belgian fries and a small salad on the side, which is the first for ages, and we spread out, cross-legged on the floor together and eat and talk.

"Eleonore, mijn kind, I want to tell you this. There are things which are going to be very different from now. Not one single person here at the zoo, nor anywhere else, is able to plan for the future. It's in others' hands at this moment, and you must learn who you can trust.

"Really, you must. And quite forget to ask why it has to be like this, otherwise there will only be disappointment. Everything will be arranged for you here at Artis, and our true Eleonore must disappear along with her past. For this time at least.

"Try, really try to be cheerful now and write me a letter for Freyja if you will, and we'll do our very best to get it to her. No promises, though. And no more map-making, it's dangerous to have plans. Everything you will leave with me."

But I'm worrying most about how I can survive without my writing, when he reaches right inside my thoughts.

"And when this is all over, Eleonore Grossman, and it will be for certain, you can have all the paper in the world the Germans have left behind, and then you will write down every single detail you remember.

"You will write and write. Never a day without writing. So that people know. Promise me."

It seems strange to make a grown-up promise, but I reply, "Promise, really promise, Gert." And it was just at that same moment where there comes into my mind an image of mumie which I just can't shake away, and I dissolve into a sea of tears, which even dearest Gert can't rescue me from.

38

Curse the Germans once, curse the Germans twice. For one, you already know of things so far. For two; who invented bureaucracy after all? And filing reports in this airless office has to be the least enviable aspect of this job by a country mile. Not that anyone alive would fight for my role.

On the other hand, I've created a whole little world between the box numbering, the box ticking, the box extemporising and myself, so that when we finally reclaim our nation, all this reflection will realise itself in the creation of an entirely new branch of philosophy; the philosophy of oppressed peoples.

Because, you will understand, the old shibboleths of collective morality, or the greater good, or whatever else in ethics, are conditional each on the assumption of unconstrained freedoms—those choices and actions of free men and women. And yet here, in this place today, any thought, or indeed any determining of events, is wholly predicated upon this one pure precept—that of zero choice. The inability not only to make a different choice, but also the freedom ever to refuse; to say no to others' choices. All implicit. So, I return to the paperwork, all too well aware that, however novel this unexplored philosophical field, it may prove far too late for we Jews.

Every piece of signed-off official work has now to wend its way to the very top of the pyramid, to the key persons whom most of us, more often than not, irreverently tag *Prof* and *Sparklers*. Childish, you might think, but Cohen is exactly that; a Prof, and I can boast that at least in a previous life we were junior colleagues together, ambitious both, and seeking advancement. Well, here we are! As for the diamond business, I have my own views, but for better or worse, a man who once held a small empire together, for that, surely, we must be at least grateful.

There's a tap at the door and how could I not smile at it's pattern? Edwin always employs the same eight determined downbeats. He claims it helps keep alive the ghost of the man whose rousing chorus 'Joy thou shining spark of God' has stirred European free thinkers for more than a hundred years. It also might serve as a warning.

The usual pleasantries observed: how is the work, how is the family? Drh Edwin Sluzker suggests we take a walk together. He clearly has something on his mind, but on mention of the Nieuwe Keizersgracht, our Jewish Council headquarters, as we climb the stairs together, there's little less likely to help calm my growing premonition that this does not always go entirely well.

We pick up a paper at the newsstand. We are still reading 'Herr Joodsche Weekblad', of course, but now largely out of loyalty to the printers employed there and our man on the corner here, whose entire income depends on it. And be aware that the journalists themselves are under no illusion as to what is permitted in the way of news. We readers must make do with a large diet of engagements and births and deaths and bar mitzvahs and, for the rest, there is only what is necessary and what is permitted.

So how delightful, don't you think, to be informed today as to the number of blankets, types of clothes and footwear, food, paper and pens you may be allowed whilst away *holidaying* on Labour Service in Germany! And please, don't forget the mandatory postcard and stamp for return home when you discover just how pleasant your surroundings are!

Black humour apart, however, and beneath Edwin's lawyerly manner, there lies a deep appreciation of nature and the arts. So he makes for a good walking companion, and it is pleasant to be out at this time in early spring with its newly pollarded plane trees, the scents and clatter of everyday Amsterdam life, its hand carts, vendors, heavy-tired vehicles, bicycles and street-cries, altogether offering an illusion that all is normal and well with the world. And Edwin's musical interests extend well beyond Beethoven. He's a fan of Debussy and Ravel, and Schoenberg, and his 12-tonal techniques that none but aficionados have any clue at all about.

But for the very first time, I notice he's shortening his steps, lagging behind. I turn around, and his shoulders have dropped. He's taking large gulps of air, he looks to be unwell.

"Edwin. Why not we take a seat for a moment," I suggest, hesitant to direct the man who, in our working life, holds so much power. Without exception though, he's gracious in his appreciation, and there's that corner bench with its oliebollen stall around the corner. We're no longer children, but—

"So, how are you feeling now?"

I scan his expression closely for any sign of false bravado, for I know he's a brave man. Minutes pass, and no reply. Quite without warning, he sobs, breaking into tears, great uncontrolled heaving of the shoulders.

I have only seen a man cry once before, and that was my father at the burial of his own adored mother. Though I was a mere child at the time and knew no better, I forever regret not having a single word then to offer in the way of consolation. Nor do I have at this moment.

He asks me to sit alongside him, and he reaches across to clutch hold of my arm, tears flowing still down his cheeks.

"Carst. I have something of grave import to share with you."

39

Dear Overgro…

I don't need to tell you the Dutch word for Great-Grandma, of course, but jeez. What is it in the mystery of your native language to complicate things so?

First things first. I sure hope this finds you a little better and that you are making the most of every moment. Fancy me giving you that advice, Oma, but *out of the mouth of babes,* etc., like they told at church, and you used to say to mum 'what has this atheist done to deserve such a righteous family?'

And second. And here you listen up, lady dude. One thing you must believe is that you did your very best for your friend, and not to have all this guilt trip hanging around. Isn't it far more the brave people who helped provide refuge who are deserving of the most attention? There, you have it.

Brutal, I know. On the subject, I imagine you remember her family name? Long time, water under the bridge, and all that, but when Irene and I took a hike around the old Jewish district, we got to see this new memorial. It's a kind of record of all the deceased who perished in the war; an extraordinary complex of brick walls, upon each of which is inscribed a single date and a single murder. If she's missing there, there's a good chance she was one of the disappeared (*submarines* or *divers*) as they are referred to here.

Now to the present. I just mentioned *ma blonde* Irene, and I have this photograph for you (enclosed). What do you think? She claims it's not her most flattering, but isn't that just a female thing, selling herself short?

But who am I to talk, like you wouldn't believe she's still waiting on my long-planned promise to take her to Artis Zoo. But what's really cool is, I really did see your wolves. A light show commemorating the trick that convinced the Germans into believing the animals were mere captives rather than the safe keepers of those hidden. All illuminated they were, huge and giant-sized, hanging amongst the trees and lurking amongst the undergrowth.

As for my studies. No, you didn't ask, but hey, I get you. Sometimes, it goes well, other times not so! Guess you felt similar too, no? When real potential turns out to be a real bummer instead. The main concern is, whatever direction I go with those times, will it really make any damn difference in the end? You tell me. So, hey I'm always desperately on the search. Depressing for sure, but, on the positives, whole bunches here do engage seriously in student politics.

So, let's stay grounded on this best friend thing, eh? Time out now. No more sentimentalising, no more moralising. Instead, I'll tell you I'm fast becoming a real dude of a Dutchman, and you'd be so proud! I make my own olliebollen, and I take my herring by its tail, as you must, and swallow it whole in one single gulp. But just how to dodge the shower of onion scraps that follow on close behind? Tell me. I need a tip.

Love Tom.
Your affectionate (g)grandson.

40

We find ourselves in a corner bar as the hubbub subsides. Families and visitors mysteriously melt away. The eager street cleaners in their bright yellow tabards crash away at stalls and stanchions, sweep and squash and bin plastic, hose pavements, and stack trailers so high that the heaps threaten to tumble.

However hard they try, they can't easily camouflage the stench of barley and hops, nor quieten the street artists who will likely continue on into the night. Just what Jos has done with his collection I cannot guess, until he tells that he was helpfully manning the stall, and this guy deserved a favour.

It's hard at first even to pick out the sounds of our voices, what with the clanging of metal on metal, the irregular whoosh of the showering of windows and unwitting bystanders. But hey, we have our drinks and Jos wants to get to know us better, and I guess we owe him, don't we?

"So, what do you remember of that night, Tom?" he asks as an opener.

It's surprising how a friendly naming helps drop one's guard.

"How do I say it? You were like welcoming ghosts. You freaking were. I was so fixated on that lunatic, I didn't even trust an instinct to turn. Jeez. I just reckon I felt like this spirit was willing us towards the trams."

"Wowee," from Irene. "That's my guy with his new-age hat on," which I don't take as exactly on side, but then comes her spoiler.

"So, don't you believe in fate, you guys? Always so weirdly rational, aren't you?"

"So what is it with life if there aren't the facts, Irene?" Jeez, that's me, just the pompous prick. There's a strained silence.

"None of your mystic nonsense here," from Jos, worrying away at the subject. "Choosing the same place and the same night, right? What's freaky about that? As if there are loads of routes back to the trams. Come on."

"And guess what?" Irene answers. "*Precisely,* the same route back. And at exactly the same time? Rational? What rational? End of—"

And that seals it now for Irene, and I guess for others too, except for me, there is another, more green-eyed explanation. We're soon back to market-trading, however.

"What I don't get, Jos, is what type buys all this—"

If there's an obvious term, I think better of it, "I guess there has to be some sort of demand out there."

"Too right, buddy. There you have it. If I were to finger all the little old gents and everyday punters who clutter around the stalls... Even the odd clergyman, would you guess? And most everyone else, from Uncle Tom Cobley and all."

I look to the others, but no joy there.

"Including, and much more on point, some serious collectors who'll pay serious money and who take time to search out the real macCoy from the crap."

We're sitting alongside a leaky door which breezes open from time to time, showering us with debris, but hey, we're lucky to claim these seats, as more and more punters retreat indoors from the market.

"But why do they want it, this stuff in particular, Jos? Stuff in particular? Why guys, why? (and, yup, I'm treading on toes.) What's with this why Tom?"

Happily, Irene flies to the rescue. "It's his family thing, Jos. You just have to run with it."

They're hanging for more, but then who else but buddy Bart steaming through the door with, "What can I get you in, gang?" and Irene, animated, leaps to her feet and hugs him.

"My mistake. Got texted earlier, and he's delayed. Should have told you all. Thought maybe a cool time for a special get-together. Celebrate our heroes. Time's right, isn't it?"

Now Jos is on his feet, hugging too, and I'm betting this will stretch into one long, long night.

41

I have tried, so many, many times, even to begin this letter for Freyja. I wonder if Gert can ever understand emotions so strong that they squeeze out everything in you that is truly human: to think, to hope, and to plan, or to pen anything other than 'I love you', over and over, if this is to be the very last message ever allowed me.

It's no good that I'm left here to myself, to 'collect my thoughts' as he says it, and no, I just cannot do this, Gert, so that is that. He is telling, at this moment, that he doesn't know the complete picture of what has taken place in the last few days, but that maybe every single Jewish person in Holland is to be taken.

Taken away, altogether put in one place. And does anyone really know why, for if they never tell you, then they really do know, don't they? Our detective work has taught us that.

It's a freezing October night, and if I stretch, I can just glimpse through the side glass of my attic refuge the unspooling of sleeping and waking mammals, of myriad reptiles and invertebrates, and just beyond, an inky canal giving back the wide expanse of a night sky. And somewhere, I know not where, a mother and aunts and cousins and all those I so dearly love, quite trapped within an uncomprehending and unforgiving world.

42

Drinks sorted doesn't come easily; it lasts an eternity. The floor is running greasy with slops, so each step is a challenge. Then there is the 'this way or that routine' to avoid headlong collisions, and yelling for attention at the bar. Also, where will Bart sit as we debate the etiquette of Irene making use of his lap, and finally opting for the edge of the table.

Now time for Irene to tell the *Grandma* tale of a family's obsession with the why question, and for Jos to reply, "What complete codswallop."

Bemused looks all around.

"It's my English word of the day. Don't you just like the sound of it? Almost Dutch?"

"Even if no one knows what the hell it's supposed to mean," observes Rene, but Jos's not done yet.

"Listen," he says, slipping into his theme. "The philosophers, the why questioners, they've all had their day," in that ballsy way that signals he's well-practiced in sounding off his opinions in a public forum. And, is he having some sort of potshot at me I wonder?

"So then, Jos. Unless we do the deeper thinking, if that's really what you're challenging; tell me, how do we learn any damn thing?" It utterly reeks of condescension, I know. Nothing much worse in a bar, even a Dutch brown bar, stained in centuries of tobacco-laden disputation. But now Bart raises a conciliatory glass.

"Proost, you wonderful people," he says, lightening the mood marvellously, and we all struggle, arms and bodies akimbo, to stretch across the table and clink glasses.

The temperature is now off the scale, and jackets, scarves and gloves are rapidly shed, all adding to the impending camaraderie. Except Jos is not quite ready yet to let it go.

"Fool's gold. Not just the philosophers but the bloody historians too."

It's no use appealing to Irene because she is studying neither, and he is at me now for sure. But then Bart—what a guy—calms by going off piste.

"So, how come you all met up here?" unacquainted as he is with Joss' market-trading line, only for yet further provocation.

"I've been selling my swastikas." He hangs, inviting outrage, but none is forthcoming.

"What's the difference, guys, you know, old coins, cigarette lighters, stamps or model trains? Or battle memorabilia. Tell me. Travelling the world or not literally stoking the boilers. Hey, we're really just playing at it. Sublimation's the name of the game. And, as it turns out, I just like playing with war."

"But…in that case—" Irene hesitates for a moment. "In that case and with your deals, Jos, aren't you worried there's so many weirdos around? Like our friend from the other night."

"Jesus. Try listening to yourselves, all of you. Who's the victim here? You're duped. Bank note collectors, urging to rob banks? Or the lighter crowd to set an inferno? Forget it. And forget swastikas too. Better puzzling your heads around the real Nazis instead."

Irene's gaze seems drilling into the side of my head, and whatever, no way can I engage the gears in my brain. Like, you got it in one. We're too many drinks into the evening by now anyways, way beyond early rounds, and no one's counting. Around the to-ing and fro-ing and jiggery-pockery we are increasingly unhinged, and *what are you really sayin'*? when we hardly know any more what we are even thinking.

At this moment, it's all clicking into *le fun* and hey, I'm jumping quite out of my skin as this one distinct image leaps to mind, in full technicolour. An image of a fully turned-out Canadian Mountie, costumed and horse-ready, as if portending my one and only certain prospect on returning back home.

43

I wait, fearful, but his news, though shocking, does not come as much of a particular surprise. Edwin is a negotiator after all, using all of his diplomatic skills, and Edwin's supreme skill lies in convincing the Germans that they have had the best of any deal agreed between them.

It is also the skill of a poker player, because from hour to hour and from day to day, it might also depend on the tone of a voice, the demeanour and the stretch of a hand or the holding of the other's eye. Sometimes even the choice of a particular brand of claret!

They will always want x number of additional Jews for their transports, so whatever the number, Edwin will halve it. Of course, that does not pass muster or please the Nazis. So, they will drop their demands, but only slightly, and then Edwin will increase his own accordingly.

As long as the final outcome betters the German demands, Edwin counts it a win. A mathematical solution to murder, as it were. It all takes nerves of steel, and God knows how it sits on his conscience. But this time around is different. The demand is dire beyond words.

He is ordered to slash the entire total of employees of the Jewish Council in half, including members of our expositor department. So far, all are protected by *bis aux weiteres,* 'until further notice'; a guarantee of safety for the time being, but not for any time longer.

His grieving is acute, "So what are we to do, Carst?" wondering out loud whether all of his equation hadn't finally run out of road.

"I'm a philosopher, Edwin. Not a magician. You know. That pen-pusher by day, maybe, but an especially deep thinker only by night."

With that slight twinkle now returned to his eye, I ask the oliebollen man if he will kindly oblige. So here are two grown men sitting on a bench and sharing a sugary snack while silently musing on which souls they will balance on the tip of a pin, before it tips either this way or that.

44

Tom, Buddy. You asked about the deal with Oma, so this old guy will begin straight out with the not-so-good news. They've discovered a failing kidney, and so she'll need dialysis. Don't freak; everyone starts with two organs, but she'll likely require multiple hospital visits and none too much hope of a long-term cure.

Naturally, we worry it might add to her confusion. We've noticed any hiccup to routine does just that, and, yeah, it's times like these I'd kill for your great aunt's advice. Your folks are really sympathetic, jeez, why shouldn't they be, but not so nearly located around the block like your man here. Means problems though. Just to remind you, in Canuck terms that's at least a day's journey each way.

Jeez. What's with this plague when the mind, once finely tuned to everyone and everything around, decides it has to lock up, and she despairs of it? You know, it's so freaking her out she sometimes shakes her whole body, rocking this way and that, like she's wrestling some demon. Frankly, she's nothing so much as a prison inmate without a release date.

Now it's out there for all to see, there's nothing much else except to play the waiting game. Rest assured, buddy. If things do take a turn for the worse, I'll shoot you a line straight away, and I'll guarantee a place right here waiting for you. Be a bit like the old days, eh? Nothing if not two kids together, they'd joke.

Sorry to be the bearer of unsettling news, though. In the meantime, I'll work on updating my tech, so contact can maybe be instant. How's Irene incidentally? Jeez. This family Oma stuff gets stuck in the brain! So don't get her sucked in to it too. As for you, hang in there and stay loose, Tom. I'll keep the old lady up to speed with all your happenings in the event you don't get the time to write, what with all that studying and all.

Fondly,
Jaap.

45

I've tried and tried, and it's just not for real anymore. Nothing more I can do. It's not like essays in class, the creation of a poem, an entry in my diary, or a last will and testament, even though that might make the best sense of all. None would prove impossible like this.

And Mr Sunier insists I must not reveal one single thing of my life or whereabouts, because he really will have this message get to Freyja, whatever it takes. And the Nazi's are now everywhere, and no one's to trust for certain.

In the end, I think back to those guessing games we played many times together, she and I; always with the help of the great Sherlock Holmes, of course, who could help solve pretty much any mystery.

Dearest Freyja. Here's one called 'Riddles'

Who am I?
Are you ready?
I have furry skin.
No. I am not a wolf. (I guessed you would say that.)
I eat mainly nuts and fruit.
I sometimes walk on all fours.
I said I wasn't a wolf, silly. I said 'only sometimes'.
Remember, we saw the Tarzan and Jane film?
I can climb. There's a clue.
Okay, you got it.
Now. Where am I?
I can see, but I can't be seen.
I am not allowed out to swing on trees. But I am safe. What now?
I have befriended a dog.

It is a Saint Bernard. It can find people, however hard it is.
One day, I hope it will get my stories to you. With love.
Always.

46

I have to tell you, I just love the feel of his lips, though I'm not sure how he rates kissing me back. Let's put it this way. Who's always the first to gently nudge away, no matter how long and passionate the embrace? And here's a thing. I love his smell just as much, if not more.

Just blindfold me and march another ten other males into the room, and I'd pick which one is Tom for sure. Part of the story as to how women bond with their newborns? But that aside, he's a solid guy, and should I really be teasing him with this knockabout stuff and Jos?

Anyway, we two are more of an item these days, or so say our best buddies. Science students like me need to be around the labs, so I'm more often than not away from the main complex. Outside of lectures, which postgrads like Tom don't have to attend, we do our odd refectory date.

"Hi, Rene. How's it hanging?" he offers in way of greeting that more often than not signals merely the briefest of pecks on the cheek.

And now less likely the three alternate pecks, as he's given up on attempting to be the native. What did I tell you? He's simply a creature of habit and more than happy with his pecks. And me replying in turn, *hanging good,* which I've learned is North American code for having nothing of substance in way of reply.

Then, "What'll you have?" from this side, because he's far more breadline than me.

I love that we're kind of cosy with each other, and that he doesn't feel obligated to charge into where he's at with his most recent work as he does with Bart. Also, he doesn't even need to utter the magic word coffee, 'cos it's a given with the Dutch, isn't it?

And his claim to be part-French simply on the provenance of where his family's tipped up (as also English, part-Dutch and part-Irish!) is, considering one thing and another, maybe why we haven't had a major fallout this far along the line. Just too much in way of cultural possibilities, so the odds are severely diminished! For sure, the odd disappointment, like we never did get to the zoo and his obsessive Oma thing, but we won't labour that for now.

Speaking of Oma, and once he's brought me up to speed, he grudgingly concedes, "You know, Rene, I shouldn't really feel guilty."

"So then don't," I reply.

"Like conversation over? Infuriating though, isn't it? A few historical facts here and there. A name we now know. A date. Anything would do."

Here we go again.

"Listen, Tom. We're stuck in circles here. And eighty years on! Eighty years. Listen to yourself. It's crazy, man."

I take his arm. "We need some air."

47

Outside is one of those damp Dutch days, when the mist still rolls in to cling to the canals until midday, and a low-slung sun shimmering onto the merchant houses, just like in those psychedelic postcards they sell in the market. And that's just where Tom's headed us. He knows we love it here, the place of his very first glimpse of Amsterdam life, and a cut-price plant that perished within days of finding its new home. These very first impressions which help shape us, tell us who we are now.

Both well-wrapped-up, it's just about mild enough to take an outside seat, and maybe another coffee. We'll see. He's learning that's pretty much a fair description of what we Dutch do with much of our time and our looted colony goods. The imbibing of coffee and the eating of sugary cakes! Mind, he's still preoccupied, my Tom. I get that look, but what the hell's going through that mind at times is impossible to fathom.

"Perhaps not the very best place to be, Rene. In this place, I mean."

Just like that. Straight out. Best to ignore him.

"It's this damn project, this country. What in hell do I know? Even this marketplace freaks me out."

He's all tensed up, and for me, I've heard too much already.

"So now you're the believer in ghosts, are you? Really, Tom? Just stop. If there'd be any single thing left of Oma's past, there's not a single survivor to help you with it."

Is he even hearing me here? What I'm telling him?

"There's this thing, Rene. Keeps coming back. This letter I mean, that she wrote long before I was born. For all her grandchildren. Straight after her one and only return visit. More in the way of an offloading of some of the stuff she'd been through, I guess. Back when Oma was due a visit, Dad would remind us of bits of that story, just to keep her sweet and connected and to show we had her beginnings in mind. Mention of a suitcase. That sticks especially. One part of the mystery I didn't put together in that whole damn story of her return to Holland many years after she'd left."

"And?"

"Perhaps there's a lead. Right here? A suitcase, Rene. And the zoo was blown up."

It's the first I've ever heard of this.

"Blown up?"

"No, no, no." He's impatient with me. "Just the bit where the Jewish I.D. cards were kept. Not the whole zoo, idiot."

48

I'm ordered to draw up a position paper. No way of sidestepping it, I'm certain. The Jewish Council has determined that only those 'essential for the organisation' will remain. And we total fourteen thousand employees! Edwin, as key player, struggles with this. He needs a firmer steer and with little time. And the one thing he and I both know is that it's the devil's choice, but, as we really are dining with the devil, isn't that exactly what a philosophical mindset is trained to address?

I've been turning over the value of *agency* more and more of late. And not just in a philosophical sense either. This way and that in my mind it goes, and with all its twists and turns.

"Give away half," they demand.

I know Edwin's inclinations well by now. He will put on that mathematical hat once again. But where, if at all, is he getting with all of that? So then. To agency. And if it's not now to consider, just when is the exact moment to reach out for what, after all, is the birthright of humans—to have and to make choices, and then to choose even to undo them?

So why not turn the tables? Turn the tables on the enemy so that you improve the odds. So we make the running. Consider your poker player. The imperative is to play the hand to the best possible effect, whatever's been dealt. First, we might consider shortening the odds. The tone of voice, the eyes, the pace of play; yes, the true professionals do all of that. So, say we are at one hundred to one on. For the card of death, that is to say. Now consider. Not a single soul knows my secret, not even Edwin. But it's clear, isn't it? Every bribe opens new opportunities, and perhaps some, or more than a few, will result in success.

If we were to learn the routes and destinations and timetables and running order of the Nazi 'freight' traffic to the east, our good friends in the RAF might then just do us a huge favour. Consider too who supplies to German headquarters in Amsterdam? Don't they just love their food and drink? All long shots, maybe, but now the odds might begin to shorten somewhat. Let's judge 80 to 1 on.

And if the Council were to ring-fence funds specifically for such trickery? And the cleverest strategists amongst us doing the planning too?

Now to the issue of weapons. We are ordered to surrender our guns and ammunition, and we encourage that surrender for fear of greater peril. But when the time comes, and because some are braver than others, why is the right time not right now? And the two main candidates for treatment: SS Hauptssturmfuhrer Ferdinand Aus Der Funten and Hanns Rauter. For who knows us better? And, by all accounts too, carry the final plan in their back pockets? By the way, we have some excellent shooters!

Agency. Agency. That's the theme, and I'm shouting it here! You see my point?

And what if you conjure up now that we simply cease to exist? Vanished into thin air. Then you truly might collapse those odds. So, go into hiding, find refuge. Okay. I insult you. I know what you will say. Fourteen thousand souls! Cloud cuckoo land.

But if this truly turns out to be the one last no-choice choice, there's absolutely no more shortening of the odds. For they've closed the whole damn book on us.

49

Hi to my dear Irene, if I might be over-familiar! Yes, as promised, this will just be between the two of us. Jaap and you. It was a real pleasure to have you write, though I can't guess just how you got to locate me! No apologies required to be concerned about buddy Tom. I know him well, better than most, and especially if it's all getting him away from his work. I have to tell you, though, that it's smack bang a family thing; this obsession with never giving up on stuff, whatever the hell else might be in the way. His Oma was precisely the same, I remember. Studying and at the same time bringing up my sister and me, and don't forget, our father was often away on exercises for months on end.

To be brief, and at risk of disappointing you, Oma can't easily bring things to her mind even from yesterday, let alone the years past. But I do keep a copy of the letter you mention, where she recounts her visit to the Netherlands, fifty years on, and a help for the kids to understand the struggles of earlier times.

It was her Uncle Paul—whom she loved as much as anyone in the world—who picked up a suitcase whilst visiting the flower market. He was somehow linked to the resistance. And her best friend's father was a watch salesman! And this case contained all his samples. Maybe it was just a boast to claim they were used to set the explosives timers that ignited the record cards of Amsterdam's Jewish population? Who knows? In 43, I think it was, but look it up, you can check it out. There's there's also mention of plans that mother and this friend drew to show the weak spots in the Artis gates and iron fencing, for speedy entry and exit if required! A number of escapers got in and out that way. Paul and her Aunt Myrese are long-time passed now, and in the end, there was an unhappy divorce, so there's a complete break in the storyline there.

Do hope this info helps calms him down, but maybe see him as a work in progress! So, let's skip to the here and now, Irene. Maybe there's something you can help me with?

The family is fretting that Oma might have less time in reasonable health than we all hope for, and I know Tom would be freaked if he missed a chance for a proper goodbye. If it's all over-dramatic, then jeez, better to be safe than sorry, eh? You get where I'm going with this?

We'd just like him close by if things turn out for the worst. Tell him no need to worry about any costs. Oma's dollars are set aside already in her will, and she has always said no reason why the kids shouldn't dig into some early if need be. She stuck firm for some time that it's best for him to struggle by on the grants, but…whatever. No pressure for a longish stayover though. The thing is that she just gets to see her favourite grandchild, one of the many in her time! And Tom knows he always has a place back home with me.

You'd be welcomed too, Irene, but 'back home' is a petite old guy's place, and me set in my ways, and there's always comings and goings as we share the care burden. Meantime, whenever there's a chance, and on her better days, I'll keep at working away at those early memories. And we now got her a whole host of hard tech so she can plug into some of the soundtrack of her former life. She's particularly enraptured by the old German marching tunes! That's all they had once upon a time, if you can imagine!

So just gentle persuasion with my buddy Tom, s'il te plais. Don't put too much pressure on him. At least, the weather back here is looking up, so he won't need that extra baggage space. But Oma says to please remind him to bring along some of your wonderful Dutch cookies!

Yours affectionately,
Jaap.

Part 2

1

A painter needs to paint. A musician needs the notes. And a writer needs to write. And brushes and instruments and emulsions and distempers, and paints, pens and paper too. Never did I ever dream how grey is a world without thoughts to be permitted to be written down. And if not so, how then to capture and unlock the mystery of yourself, let alone the mystery of others?

And then, eureka. I have it. The brain can write, can't it? Every moment, every day, the brain is an obsessive writer. And is a good listener too! So, here's my brain letter to my dearest friend.

Dearest Freyja

Right here is safety, during daylight hours anyway. So many people, just part of the crowd. I don't need to travel far to my workplace; just around the corner, for yes, I am a 'little 'teacher again. And when I say 'little', I mean for the very little and even the littlest!

If I ever become a mother one day, this will be the very best preparation of all. Also, you need to know there are many heroes around me who would win any cycling competition you could ever invent. And, for that, they risk far more than a fall and a scraped knee.

It will please me if you don't worry too much that I lack friends. There are many here, and mostly a little older than me, true, but they are patient and kind.

It's a long working day, and afterwards, especially in the winter months, I must be more careful. You could never guess who I am now, however hard you tried, but it's probably all I ever wanted. And I hope we too, one day.

P.S. The great Sherlock Holmes himself would never get to the bottom of a brain letter; however hard he tried.

2

Is this history repeating itself? I'm on a journey bound out of Schiphol for Canada, without the faintest idea how Oma made it back all those years ago. A troop ship, maybe?

Seven hours ahead of me, mobile set to aeroplane mode, movies scrolled through, seat straps long released, and time to dream. Not that my dreams are ever deep, but at some point they are clearly interrupted. There's a sensation of movement around me, and I swiftly grab and check out my mobile. Already two hours in and my neighbour is on her feet.

"Excuse me. Sorry to disturb you," she says as she sidles past.

It's the usual flying business, of course. The woman's smart, in a fussily dressed way. And she takes my reply, "No problem, ma'am," as an invitation to strike up conversation once she's settled back.

"You must be Canadian?" I'm asked.

I must admit a small twinge of guilt, being so entirely in my head from the start that her existence hadn't so much as registered. I turn sideways for a handshake.

"Tom," I offer.

She, in reply "Margot. Pleased to meet you."

The Dutch inflexion is clear. It's her first visit to Montreal, but not to the country, for like many Netherlanders, we Canucks will always be viewed as liberators.

"May I try a question for you, Tom? You'll think obvious I know. But what would you say I should see as a first-time visitor?" If a next-seat neighbour implies any kind of obligation at all, then a complete lack of tour guide credentials shouldn't hold a person back.

"I guess it depends whether you're in the city or travelling on," I say, which, precisely at the moment of telling, seems unnecessarily unhelpful. For sure, she's making small talk, but jeez, advice is all she's about after all.

"Well, hey-ho. I guess if I say everywhere and anything, that wouldn't help one jot, would it? But it's a fact. You're really spoiled for choice over there." She waits, anticipating more.

"So, I imagine you wouldn't want to zipline down by the water? Or take a turn on the Ferris wheel?"

Happily she's quite unfazed.

"Is that in way of suggesting an old spring chicken can't have fun," and on that teasing note, we appear to have broken the stranger-stranger barrier.

"Apologies, Margot. Ignore me. It's just this guy and his many quirks. I'm much more confident muddling through my research papers."

"You're a student Tom? Well, just fine. So, try me with something a tad cultural." I relax.

"Sure. So, the Musee des Beaux Arts. Why not kick off there? They say it's the oldest in Canada, and then what? I don't know, maybe a shot at the Botanical Gardens and the Biosphere on the artificial island."

I'm quick running out of gas with the big sites though, and this feels sheer drone, so I add, "If I'm honest, there's way too much out there to explore."

She is rummaging in her bag, searching for something on which to scribble. I offer the pencil which sits alongside the menu list, and, for sure, if its foodie suggestions she wants, it has to be downtown Mile End any day.

"Cool, beyond belief Mile End. All things Italian, Greek and Portuguese there, if you're prepared to try stuff out. Truly amazing. Just pig out on the lamb moussaka, the red snapper, the—"

Seriously, that exhausts my grown-up food repertoire, for down-at-heel undergrads don't get to fine dining every day. And it's been a while since I was back home, and then more than likely it's tourtière or maple taffy or beavertail all the way. And she'd need a translator as well as a guide for all that!

I'm grateful for a change of direction, though, as Margot's much superior run-through of Amsterdam places connects us to the more familiar, and the journey soon speeds after that.

I like that she's curious about my dalliance with the Netherlands and, of course, not so long before the Oma story comes out with her current ill-health, and much of the rest from long ago. Especially the zoo sheltering the fugitives among the animals, which she insists she's never heard of. And, of course my even newer-found dalliance with the city and Irene.

This is so much easier than directing a stranger around a vast city, I'd say. And as good a listener as I need.

"So when it comes down to it, count yourself a lucky boy, Tom. Pretty much this far in life anyway. So sorry for your Oma, though."

It feels we've talked ourselves out, and it's not long before she picks up her reading once more.

3

Brain letters needn't be so secret after all. The Nazis can't read minds. They can't know what we want. Who we want to love. Yes, they can try and force it out of you, but if you have a reason to live... And, being hidden at night, and having lots of thinking time... I have lots of thinking time.

Like thinking back to what Mumie and Papi have taught me and what I have learned. Yes, I know that I love them the best of all, but I love my friend too, and why can't that be the best love also?

Someone said that you have to fall out of love with your parents one day, and your feelings for your friends, so that you can leave behind all those ties. Then you can love your new found lover the very best of all. Well, it's a long time to wait just to find out if it really is true, isn't it? And what are you missing in the meantime?

I know I couldn't write this in my diary, even if I were allowed paper and pen once again. And then that comes to the matter of secrets. I think about this a lot. Do secrets ever really get written down? And if not, where are they stored?

There's much talk of plans all around me now, even though I don't know anything for certain, and I shouldn't even glimpse into the future if each day is to be my last.

4

I'm pissed that there's not a window to gaze through, and flight-trackers disappoint regarding the true lie of the land and my neighbour is deeply absorbed in her reading and jeez, I can't decide on a movie I might like and I worry about Oma. But then the clattering of the galley staff is holding out the promise of refreshment to come.

It's some time before we're interrupted by a flight attendant asking for our meal order. As we consider our menu cards, Margot says with a smile, "This is the only good that comes out of it, Tom. Fly LKM and you eat Indonesian," me meanwhile observing the merits of rending, samba and vegetable atjar, and would you know it, I am like a true Dutchman once more.

Whilst we wait, I ask what she's reading.

"Whenever I visit a new place, I choose a book that opens a window." She shows me the cover, and I'm none the wiser. "It's a special story for me, Tom. All about a family fleeing Vietnam for Montreal in the 1970s. I'll read it whilst eating pho in one of your city restaurants."

And then she adds, "We all have our stories, I guess. You and me both."

There's something unspoken in this, and I wonder whether I haven't been just too much carried away with myself and Oma on this journey. She seems to want to tell in any event.

"In case you're wondering, I'm a child of the colonies. I guess we don't get to hear quite so much about that in Amsterdam these days? It's all pretty much Eurocentric now, isn't it? World War Two and all that. School curriculum, TV shows. We can't put it to bed."

I'm loath to admit that I'm so stuck on grandma's story that most else in Holland's past has completely passed me by.

"For me, both grandparents out there were responsible for some bigger things," she says. "Never quite sure precisely what, but part of the administration in Indonesia clearly."

"Not a charmed life by all accounts, whatever some say, being neither native, nor European either. Identities moreover that were so rigid to escape that you can imagine the feeling of the void of never ever quite belonging. A population seven times that of Holland, bigger even than your Canada, Tom. Even so, you quickly learn to know your place. And later, much worse to follow."

Our cardboard packs arrive, and it's some time before we get to return to our conversation.

"You were mentioning, Margot. You didn't quite wind up your colony story."

She hesitates.

"Just say, if you don't want to hear this Tom. I know you are being polite."

"Jeez. Not at all. It's all new to me. Just shows how narrow my education is. Go right ahead."

"So then; being Indo-Dutch that is so easily noticed. Your life as a young child becomes a struggle: name calling and bullying and often feeling alone. So, for my parents…that must have been…Anyway, they all had to get out pronto back in the day. A civil war and hatred, especially toward anyone they saw as on the occupier's side."

"Worse of all, the Dutch back home, half-starved by the Germans, well, naturally, they resented us. Even for the little in the way of recompense they received for generations of supporting their empire."

And then, somewhat sadly, "It can slip down the generations, Tom, you know. Do you understand that? So, look. Don't fret over much about your Oma. You're far too young for that kind of thing. She lost a friend, that's all. Nothing more."

I'm almost embarrassed now for my trifling story, but she adds, "It's the sheer hypocrisy which irks me. You know, afterwards. Always afterwards. Those who'd betrayed, took the bribes or whatever. What right had they to judge others?"

I am floundering here, and I can't think of anything to say, except, ridiculously, "My Oma was rescued by a soldier."

Margot, apropos of nothing at all, replies, "A soldier is a soldier is a soldier."

5

Tom is with his parents for just a few days, but I am missing him already, and though it's only forty eight hours, I just have to get to him. Right now! It's so weird, this tiny figure on the screen, but has he lost a single thing in the chat department? Absolutely no way.

"Don't have a clue about the 'soldier is a soldier is a soldier', Tom, but the Indonesia stuff, that I can do. There was a war with them, soon after peace was declared, with the Germans gone from Holland."

"Everyone there wants their independence now, and it all gets a bit dirtier after that. But be warned though, it's still something of a sore subject in Holland. Even seems to hang on still."

"After all those years, Rene? Jeez, that's plain crazy."

"And your fascists too. Even longer, yes?"

"Okay. Okay, Rene. But so sad that this nonsense doesn't just outgrow itself, don't you think? Like lots else, I mean. What the hell's evolution for if nothing gets a deal better?"

He's coming on strong now, not so much the cool history guy, so I put him straight, "Maybe because it still works, Tom, and can you really kill an idea? It's rare that an entirely brand-new version comes along, and then those that come after can catch it too, and there it goes; twice over. It's a disease isn't it."

That appears to settle that, and now he's most keen to update me on Oma, whom he gets to see in the hospital when he's finally done with his folks. Yes, a freaky way to describe family, don't you think?

"It's not that we don't rub along, Rene, it's just effing difficult, having done your own thing for so long." Then, and did I really get to hear this? "I guess our own thing now."

He's uncomfortable with sentiment, my guy, and he needs reassurance.

"Tom, I really do miss you, you know."

He's missed me too, so can I risk just a tiny mention of Jos? Gentle now. "You remember the guy with the tattoos?"

"You still see him?"

"You're kidding, aren't you?" As we're in the same faculty building, that's hardly a stretch. "Just be cool now Tom. It's about how it all kicked off. Him and his swastika thing. Or don't you want to know?"

Red rag to a bull with Tom. He just hates to be out of the loop, like the cat who's always hanging around the place, lapping up the spilt milk.

"From way back, his parents had this family friend who'd always been full of the nationalistic nonsense. At that time, our dear Wilders was just a councillor in Utrecht, and coincidentally, that's where they went on regular family visits.

"Jos would be entertained with the usual about replacement theory, you know, turning the white world black or some such, and the enfeebled Dutch blah, blah, blah. He would wonder just what they had in common, his family and theirs and why they stuck with him.

"So, I'd have just ignored it all. Grown-ups can talk such crap," says Tom.

"Hey. Listen to you, nerd. Try to imagine. He's a young kid; he doesn't know much and doesn't want to upset the folks most of all. Wouldn't you be the same? Even when he tries to argue back, the guy just won't listen. Treats him like a complete idiot. Always shouted down. Anyway, he has good Muslim friends at school and—"

I'm not sure Tom is still hanging in there.

"Are you still in for this, Tom?"

"All ears, Rene. All ears."

"So, to cut a long story short…there was this big bust-up and he refused to go with family visits anymore. Anyway, his folks wouldn't let it go, so he mugged up on everything he could find. The Nazis, the eagle and the symbols and all that, and came up with this wheeze.

"The very next time they returned to visit this guy, he penned two small swastika marks between each thumb and forefinger. And…they're all sitting around this guy's table, and all quiet from Jos until the guy notices the tattoos. Though he's curious, that really throws him.

"You know where this symbol comes from?" he asks Jos.

His mother, trying her best to cool things down, says," I don't like him scrawling all over his fingers and—"

Tom interrupts, "Jeez. So, what made him add in the others?"

Tom needs work, I can see that.

6

I don't really remember exactly back to a hospital ward, except there are the beds you might expect and here, right above, silent TV monitors flickering between programmes. And worried visitors and nurses carrying and fetching, and a low reverential murmur you get in a holy place.

Also, a whole collection of what appear to be 50s-era computer cabinets each with their whirling discs, circulating blood. Each patient, like Oma, is linked to the boxes via plastic tubing from arteries in the wrists, chest or neck and, as this is a long procedure, books and newspapers are scattered bedside, crosswords and word puzzles attempted.

I'm pretty relieved to see that Jaap's already here. A long hug, first granny and then Jaap. After all, when was it we were last all together? And Oma tells me for the hundredth time that she's pleased to see her favourite grandchild.

She also tells me that she gets much pain from having to stay on her back for so long. I clearly see her agitation in that continuous tossing and turning, which Jaap tells can only be calmed by heavy doses of medication.

My arrival has engineered his familiar broad smile, and as these are 'hellishly long sessions', he suggests, why not I'll be back before grandma needs fetching home? We'll have plenty catch-up time in the next days in any event.

Although I've much to tell Oma, and she's especially curious about Irene, it's all pretty much one-way traffic from the start, until the moment she takes hold of my arm and doesn't seem willing to let loose.

"I didn't want to have him, you know that Tom?"

I fear the worst. Our first time together for a long while, and what exactly had been Jaap's warnings about her state of mind?

"The baby, I mean." It all comes blurting out.

"We didn't know much about sex in those days. Can you believe it? But I just knew one thing for sure. I needed your grandpa so much that it was the most loving and natural thing we could do."

It's as if she has been saving this up for a whole lifetime, and she's reached bursting point, and I'm the one least equipped to know quite where this should go next.

"I'm listening, Oma. I'm all yours."

It's the best I can do, and I shift my position around the bed just slightly so that we're fully face to face. I gently loosen her grip, take her hand in mine, and promise that it will be our secret, ours alone.

"I'm not finished, Tom. I was ashamed at first—I'm sure you will understand—and then embarrassed, naturally. Maybe it just didn't seem that these things should happen to girls like me. And then you can't stop it. It's like an express train, time whooshes by, and is there anything in the world you can do about it?

"The worry about neighbours and your parents' friends and all, and what they think. Most of all, your parents don't want any mention of it.

"Then they arrange for you to go away somewhere, and that is the moment when you must decide this little person inside of you counts for more than any of them and their betrayals. The ones who are supposed to love you the most."

I can see the tears and the emotion of reliving her long-ago past leaving her quite exhausted and the best I can do at this moment is to tell her I understand everything, and there is no shame.

She's drifting in and out of naps now, and I can pay closer attention to the appearance of the Oma I've known so well these years. As far back as I remember, she's fitted the *well-filled* lady description, that family tag that insinuates more Dutch than Canadian, and more than anything, thanks to those blond, clog-shod images on tourist mugs. But the soft folds of arms, face and neck are now shrinking quite away from the limbs beneath, and redrawn with a certain gaunt aspect which, at the very first glance, comes as a shock to me. And her head of snowy hair is much reduced to the point where it hardly makes camouflage of her skull anymore. But she's still my very own Oma, for sure. How could she not be?

She's fallen into a half-doze now, her breathing shallow, so I chance to lean across the turned-down counterpane to retrieve my shoulder bag, and a moment to think. At once I'm struck by the impact of the bright ward lighting on her wrists and arms, her sleeves rolled back and the skin highlighted, snake-like with interlocking and meandering patterning, as if fashioned by an artist and I'm immediately brought back to that very first glimpse of Jos's tattoos in the restaurant when I simply couldn't take my gaze away, even though he'd most likely noticed my staring. At the same time, I recall last evening's video call when Rene had done her best to drag me out of my ignorance concerning the swastika symbol; that hooked cross found even in pre-history, symbolising divinity and spirituality.

Like lots else, the Nazis cleverly appropriated it, choosing to link chance similarities between Asiatic and German languages and icons found on pottery and ivory figurines as confirmation of a common Aryan, god-like super-power.

A number of Hanny's archives show mass rallies of German youths formed up into gigantic ranks, mirroring the arms of the symbol and whose image Herr Hitler had decreed could only be allowed by permission of the state. And also affixed to countless flags, of course, of symbolic red and black, quite exceptional for political parties of the time.

And if it should have occurred to me before, it's clear that a symbol can be read for virtually anything at all, from the sheer beauty of the form itself, as much as its sentiment of strength and determination.

And then again, it's a somewhat indented, chopped-up image, as if somewhat smashed and scary, and doesn't it depend on who does the reading, after all? I'm all over the place with this.

Later, I scroll down Google on ancient symbols, and come across the three-cross motifs of Amsterdam; a protection from fire, floods and death, with equally significant potency. Much less bother if Jos had chosen that symbol in preference!

7

The sand is warm and silky, and there are tingles between the toes which, by instinct, turn upwards to rebalance this body in motion. The flags flutter, and it's the flutter I feel rather than the flutter of the flags.

All is azure, and it's quite painted over the clouds. There is no horizon except the water holding down tight against the sand. And no sun in the heavens, except for its imprint, which is a brilliant slash, joining the land and sea together like a paper clip.

Nor does this air carry any scent at all, and we are quite alone. I know this, for there are no sounds out there, yet there are feelings inside where now all sound resides. And I sense the beating of a heart right up into the delicate folds of an ear, and its folds like a petal and a loose curl of silk that I could slide right down.

And the dull ache for what might be, and the frisson of uncertainty and all that is unknown. We lie down together in the sand. We two and our brain letters, which are all we have left of each other.

8

I have this fantasy. Maybe the best way I can surprise Tom on his return is to find out more about Eleonore. I know that comes across as Princess Charming and her Knight in Distress, but I really felt for him earlier. Also worrying seriously about his fixation on this one particular thing.

Maybe it all makes some sort of sense if, as he's always claimed, he's a little light on family, except for loads of cousins of course. But then his grandparents on Jaap's sister's side did move away to England for a long period, with only his mother returning after divorce. He doesn't speak much about it. Then a new family was formed, which is maybe why he's so close to his Oma.

So why not give this a punt? Nothing to lose, is there, and maybe some small detail to gain? Plus we know of the new memorial wall and its location, and Jos has offered to help with this. And don't tell me it would be simpler still to check the computerised records, for every name on every brick is logged there after all, but what are you suggesting? Okay, it's a day out with a guy. And how could Tom ever know?

The wall harvests the raindrops on each exquisitely-engineered brick, and Jos is kneeling close to scan the family names, but no Eleonore so far, and we have nothing yet of her family name.

"Heh, you." Jos has his hand still on the wall, and it's clearly a shout in our direction.

"You," a woman's voice repeats urgently. "What are you doing here?" The woman stands firm and is loudly demanding an answer.

At first, I'm embarrassed for him, as there are many around who now can't fail to notice, and she won't be calmed. He gets to his feet.

"Just tell me. What are you doing here? Don't hide."

A number of bystanders, clearly wishing to be somewhere else at this moment, begin to move away. But Jos approaches her directly, taking her by the arm, and, quite calmly, "I assure you, mevrouw. I have no intention to offend, and I can quite understand your feelings. And if you wouldn't mind—" drawing her away from me,

"Perhaps we can find a corner somewhere and I'll do my best to explain?"

She hesitates, seeming unconvinced.

"Please. Do come. I'd like to help."

So incredibly polite, so charming is Jos that the woman appears momentarily disarmed as he steers her away.

I stand stock still for some minutes, not sure what to do. But now I text him rapidly, *at the Plantage*, and determine to walk to the restaurant three streets distant. Puzzling as to what he can possibly say, I head off.

It's only a few minutes' walk, and as always, it's crowded here. So, I perch on a stool at the end of the counter, and worry at just how I might have helped smooth things along. I get the woman's rage. Clearly, I do, and maybe? Maybe what? I'm the world's best at revisioning events, but when things are happening so fast… Moments can't be stretched endlessly to allow thinking time, can they? But hey: he knows where I am and I order us coffee and apple cake, willing him not to be long. The waitress says that they are a little slow today.

"It happens," she tells me without explanation.

I'm still pondering how Jos keeps things so together. At the one minute calm, and then restless. I read my messages over and wonder if I should retrieve my steps and offer a hand, but perhaps not so long now if he's on his way. I'm also thinking twice about my Oma plan. If we find the name, is it game over for Tom? Or will he want to remake her journey and her fate in his imagination, and do whatever he's driven to go out and do? And if not, what then? I'm struggling here, nowhere near a miracle solution, when Jos appears at the entrance. No signs of fluster at all.

"So tell me," I ask when he's cosied down, our cake and drinks settled, and he spoons the slagroom from the top of his cappuccino and takes giant gulps from the crust of the cake.

"For sure, she wasn't easy, Irene. It had been all over the press. Some bastard desecrated a synagogue wall in Utrecht with swastikas, and it had made headlines. Lots of letters, TV and stuff. So, it was all too raw for her. I guess my being Canadian took some of the heat out of it.

"And then, I filled her in with my family thing and their friendly fascist friend. Also, how at first the guy just couldn't fathom me, like when he asked my plans for after leaving school and I told him something obscure like, 'I'm hoping to visit Tutenkarmen to see the stuff they stole from the Jews, or to check who paid for the treasures of Islam?"

"And…No, I really didn't tell her all of that, but hey, for sure, I eventually had become confrontational with this guy, and I wouldn't stop until I'd extended the swastika count a little more until finally, he and I would remain sulkily silent, and I wasn't allowed to visit ever again. And after that, I grew to like the patterns I had created. And really got into tattoo."

"You were telling me about the woman, Jos, weren't you? Was she convinced?"

"I guess, especially when I added that you were there, looking to trace your Jewish relatives."

Jesus Mary, I can't believe him.

"But that's a f…lie, Jos. Why the hell did you do that?" I'm angry with him.

"Come on, Irene. Don't be such a dupe. Just chill. It all depends on what you call a lie."

"A lie's a lie. Okay."

"And is a swastika always a swastika?"

I'm puzzled. And not for the first time with Jos.

"Look, the trick they have always done is to conjure through association. Swastika usually means strength and power; certainly, it did to the Nazis. So, if you turn the meaning upside down, you begin to challenge the force of the symbol. Like the hippies took that symbol too. For them, it was a symbol of love. It forces people to think, recalibrate and maybe helps change minds. That subversion. Anyway, can you honestly swear that you don't have a single Jewish ancestor? You know, from way back?"

I'm not happy. This is Jos at his most infuriating. Is the man ever remotely straightforward about anything? But I'm going to credit him with one thing. Not only did he step up for the search, which unhappily produced not a trace of Oma's friend, he has asked if I would like to go with him to the zoo.

9

Gran and I haven't had much in the way of uninterrupted conversation, given the arrival of anxious visitors, the fetching and carrying, and the reordering of seats. Nor by the whirring machines, which frequently go crazy. There is nothing here settled, it's all skirmish.

You have frequent alarms, all red or orange flashing lights and buzzers and a staff member who, with a single switch of a toggle, preserves momentary calm. I'm somewhat surprised to see one patient, distracted from his regular pursuit of crossword and sudoku, calmly leave his bed to cancel his own alert alarm!

But there is one advantage to all this; the stretch of time needed by a dialysis patient easily extends into hours and gives me space to think. That stranger on the plane has perchance launched me into weighing relativities. Hell, Einstein, no less. So, tell me, which histories do or should take precedence? And if things really only make best sense if grounded in their particular times, what then? And if I'm wrong about the swastika thing? After all, a cross has inspired millions across millennia, so why shouldn't a swastika evoke fear and pain for eternity? And will I complete this damn project in the time frame and what of the opportunity cost and my shaky love life? Why not serve oliebollen and spend my whole time with Irene for the rest of my days?

And really: in any event, does my Oma have any place in all this grand theorizing after all? Was she just an unwitting agent in the grand march of history, did she shift the dial one jot, deflect history, albeit by a fragment, or can whole swathes of individuals be written out?

Sure, she had her share of adolescent fancies and disappointments, but was that any more than a childish love affair, and then all over when her soldier, the true love of her life, appeared on the scene? And for him, was war much more than a thrilling adventure, albeit mighty dangerous, for the son of an iron ore miner who had never been out of René-Lévesque, let alone journeyed into Montreal.

I've worried away at 'the soldier is a soldier' remark and had texted Bart.

'You can't put a cigarette paper between soldiers who, by chance or circumstance, are on the winning side, and those who are the losers,' he replies. 'And as the taste for war increases, a descent into barbarism. And not just for the fighters. After all, isn't a soldier just a trained killer?'

It's not a take grandma might have on all of this. Jack was her rescuing hero, and retribution for what friends and family had done to her. And isn't it much more likely that right now my questioning is no more than me struggling with the bigger contingency question, for it's a sure thing a little lonely out here, and I guess just feeling sorry for myself, citing your honour, unconfirmed jealousies (just *where* is Jos right now) and a worrying for funds as the grants dry up. More to the point, where precisely am I with this Irene person at this particular moment in time?

So, I message her:

'Oma sends her love' (has she? No matter). I'm really missing you (I am, but more likely I'm worried about you—and him). I'll be back soon (really, can't be sure). Can you hop on a plane? (unlikely, she doesn't have much more in readies than I).

Then I try out various other deceptions that trick us through the days. I try to picture her, but she's slipping away. Yes, she's medium height, the hazel eyes are still there and not *le blonde,* though I call her that. And then, determinedly and with real effort, but now for myself, Jesus Mary. Just cheer up, you loser.

After all, I have a visitor pass to the university right here, so I can squeeze in some relativities on homegrown fascists, and say howdy to friends and relatives yet unsearched. But surely, most ways, the present deal is I'm bidding out a kind of extended farewell to Oma and all our memories together. And happily Bart's doing okay; still lost in medieval Europe and likewise looking for some girl to save his life. Any girl at all, he's cool with that. And Hanny's son, Harvey, I imagine, is happily perfecting his English and no doubt his greater understanding of Spinoza.

And I'm awakened from my reveries by grandma and her very first words, "What news of Eleanore?"

She dreams a good deal these days.

10

Amsterdam itself hasn't been bombed, it's true, but you don't need to be told about the monotonous booming from our nearest town here to understand these things, and the obvious lightening in the steps of everyone around, and the rumours swirling alongside here and everywhere.

But first, you will want to know more about that final journey, naturally. When I left the zoo.

For myself, I didn't have a return ticket, but my travelling companions certainly did. After all, the animal dung that helps fertilise the crops on which the cattle feed will, in turn, need be returned in the form of their meat.

Without any doubt, that was the stinkiest journey ever undertaken, and it felt never-ending. And as for my arrival, my guardian angels, who at this time for safety must remain nameless, they will one day, with many others, populate entire history books and enjoy the praise of all nations.

The stink once here didn't improve all that much. But now it's the sweet-sour chalky aroma of dairy, and the slippery, twice-daily battle with teats that seem to spring away like rubber bands, however hard you try. Once balanced precariously on my stool, 'Seize them, just seize them,' I'm instructed, as if the mere act of telling will magic them towards me.

And whenever I near the cow sheds, I find myself engaged in a relentless daily skirmish with the aggressive geese. They hiss and stubbornly refuse to move aside until I brandish my boot in their direction and express my frustration.

You just wouldn't ever envy my 'fashion sense' now, but absolutely no photographs allowed, which can only be a good thing. My new family name couldn't have come more easily, as has the minor flipflop of religion, less so the growing pains of this body, which is now turning as messy as my existence. And the lack of...Except this is not the place for that now.

And it's the 'when' questions that truly haunt me here; not yet to be shared with you, dear diary, but raging and burning daily into the mind, often at the most unguarded of moments. And this particular one above all. When will I ever again sit alongside my dearest friend, my family and school friends all together, and laugh and embrace and yes, even cry? Then will it be for ever and ever, tell me? which is in all the very best children's stories, of course.

11

Dzieki Bogu. Close to the bridge at last. We're almost there. Not what was hoped for from the earliest days of training, but every second of exploding mortars, of rattling machine-gun fire, is a calculated battle between life and death. And then a massive blast, a tearing of eardrums, exploding, searing pain, and our Polish heaven reclaims another of its own.

12

I've become curious about this ancestry thing. Nothing at all to do with Jos's taunt about how can we know every detail about our heritage, of course. Nor Tom's about my imaginary German roots! But he's right. Fischer is a common enough European name after all.

Luckily, the national archives displayed now on my computer are a veritable encyclopaedia of births, places, family lines, and generations. And now I have a little time, why not dig a little deeper? Admittedly, I've rarely thought seriously back beyond my parents' generation, most likely because, growing up, I had this morbid fear of the complete emptiness of a world that existed before any of us. Just grey and stretching endlessly, it seemed. Likewise, the idea of death terrified in the same way; being dead after the *not dead* time.

At university, I read an English writer who perfectly sums up my dread. 'Not to be here/Not to be anywhere/And soon…nothing more true.' Admittedly, I skipped the 'Nothing more terrible 'because that's for when I get old! But I was much happier to trust in the land of the living. So; tangible objects—oh, so fine, solid and extant. They were my comfort zones. Often, I drove everyone crazy with the what and where and when, as if fixing these landmarks might themselves prevent everything from quite ghosting away. Was that before, or after? Just fill in the gaps with me, and I'm fine.

Fortunately, everywhere around me, always the reminders of solid items as if they represented living: the dykes, canals and windmills and the heavy-sailed boats with their flat bottoms and their *wings* for steering and balance. Now factor in ale houses, civic halls, markets, and, last of all, just shake in the scents and sounds. And, as I was getting older, yes, many more of the bigger questions too, but which now don't frighten, as once upon a time with my fears.

But isn't it this flickering screen before me and this technology—with its vast collections of data and algorithms and messaging, which offers something equally tangible—our greater links to those pasts which existed even before our grandparents' times? For, excepting now-fading photographic prints, diaries, letters and family folktales, our own longer history is largely lost.

But at this moment, scratching away at the surface of newly discovered rabbit holes into the *way back*, and I can see how people are so easily sucked in. A minority sport has now become a tsunami. And familiar though I am with Tom and Jaap's own accounts of Freyja's return to Holland; her rediscovering her brave and favourite aunt, and her reacquaintance with the story of those hidden in Artis Zoo and hunted by the Nazis, what of Oma's own connection to *her* past? To *her* parents and grandparents and whoever came before. And is it mere curiosity, a tedious life away from Tom, that is tempting me, as so many others, beckoning me on to make that click to the next screen and then the next and the next, and to offer the subscription when prompted, and finally to sign up for a DNA test to discover if I really am related to Rembrandt! No. That's sheer invention, but you can see how it goes, can't you?

The one thing I guess, though, is that, like most women in Holland, by tradition his Oma will have taken her new husband's family name on marriage. On occasions though, and when answering the medic's routine questioning for assessing memory, Tom says she offers her birth name. The premier of Canada-yes, she's okay with that, her age and place of residence likewise, but not always Frejya Wargers. It's the child she remembers.

And so, eyes firmly fixed on the screen, time easily loses meaning, and here I am, transported back to the people and their connections of some eighty years past. And right there, easily spotted, are Oma's father and mother's titles, with city, district and house number of the street, their dates of birth and religion and directly beneath is written the child Freyja. But that name doesn't sit alone. There is another registration, and this is directly above. The name of a second child; a child one year older than Freyja!

13

They are waiting for me at Schipol; Rene, Bart and a girl I don't immediately recognise.

"Gunilla." Bart steps forward. "Say hello to Tom."

She offers me a winning smile, and I see that she is a member of the gang. She knows to kiss three times on the cheeks.

Rene says, "And what about me?"

So we embrace, and they all applaud. There's much to catch up with, and I suggest a bar stop, which is also a Dutch way. I learn that Gunilla is a Swedish student and she and Bart have only just met, but he's been 'completely blown away'. He will put his doctorate on hold, and they will travel the world together. Jeez!

I admit to a slight fit of pique that all of this happened without a whisper, and me being kept schtum despite all the texts and contacts. But hey, give them the benefit of the doubt. I'm under grandmother pressure, and they understand she's unwell.

And put on one side there's just a stirring of envy that now he's shaken free of deadlines to be met, sources to be pinned down, and seeming contrary conclusions to be balanced. But if he's happy.

An unexpected playful punch to my tummy muscle from Rene, a first for me.

"So, it wasn't Rene who brought you back, Tom?"

She's back to the brave Canadian warrior routine, which is beginning to go down like a lead balloon, but hey, it's all new to Gunilla. Still, there's lots of joshing and the joyous stuff of our togetherness, before Gunilla says, "You haven't seen the new baby, Tom." I wonder for one moment whether I'm out of yet another loop when she ushers us through the lounge into the parking lot, and there's a shiny, though somewhat beaten-up VW van. After much mutual admiration, we all pile in for the trip to wherever.

The springs are shot, the seats are hard, and it doesn't ride well, and I fear for their future and for their travels. Much too-ing and fro-ing along the way. First Montreal, then Amsterdam, and now Stockholm. We're headed further out of the city by now, to a sliver of waste ground to park up, which appears to be a kind of graveyard for faded wrecks of vans and automobiles and much detritus.

"And the beers are cheaper here," boasts Bart, dragging us around a corner to their new favourite place, but now too late for us to benefit hereafter, darn it. But we do get a little more time to catch up and even mull over early plans for goodbyes.

14

I'd been struck as we'd journeyed through the city, it felt like Amsterdam was now a place quite shrunk away; its streets narrower and more crammed than I remembered, it's buildings more populous, and with little room to breathe. I imagined that without its canals to act as markers, this place would be as higgledy-piggledy as a scene from a Brueghel painting.

In the tram on the way back to the city, I ask Irene if there are Brueghel's in the galleries here. She doesn't know, but soon, she is excitedly updating me on everything we left hanging.

"It was all of a sudden, Tom, quite out of the blue. The Bart and Gunilla thing. Instant karma, if you ask me. We didn't want to bother you with all your Oma problems."

Not a mention of Jos throughout, and as we hit a tight bend at speed, we are thrown close together against the pitch of the bucking tram. In my imagination, I magic away all of our friends, Oma, and study, and every other thought in my head. At this particular moment, I want more than anything in the world to be entirely alone with this one person I truly believe I love.

15

Dearest Irene,

Montreal.

Let's cut to the quick. I'm sure you're right in your decision not to let on to Tom about your family discovery. Most likely, some forgery was behind it, just as there were false identity cards and lots of other invented documents floating around at that time.

And sure, the Germans were sticklers for their paper and records. Knowing Tom, he simply couldn't let this news go, and he's also seriously uptight that he's in a bind with his research, and lots else going on in his life at this moment. Deep down, he has this notion that his supervisor—who's the real deal with sources and referencing and advice and so forth—is at bottom convinced that the Dutch have only themselves to blame for so many bloody fascists there in the first place! So that appears to be twin tracks! And no darn help to Tom either. Best not breathe a word of that to Hanny. They say the whole war issue is still somewhat dynamite back with you.

Farewells weren't a bundle of joy either, Irene. His Oma didn't want him to leave, of course. His sister had hiked up a distance to see him, and why couldn't he stay just a little longer and so it went. Jeez. In the end, I simply paid for another departure date to help get him out of the place.

Good for you too, that you kept him in the dark about his buddy throwing his whole research project whilst he was away. Even more reason for glum on Tom's part. And watch out, Irene. Something else. Tom's a real jealous type! Do I need to tell you that? So, here's the score. What say you cut him as much slack as you can? He dotes on all his friends for sure.

And get him away from this whole damn ridiculous thing of searching out a stranger from eighty years ago, like it's some sort of family redemption deal. You bet I blame my sister for this, who made the whole family line stick with the God project way beyond its due end date. And you know what mother made of religion, don't you?

It was for sure the Lutherans that kicked off the whole damn Jewish business in the first place!

Your new friend,
Jaap

16

The English East Midlands is a long way from Warsaw, but who would disagree that war is the best guarantor of broadening your travel horizons? On the other hand, we're still in recovery from the harsh climate of Scotland and the frustrations of numerous battle opportunities so far denied us. Up there, our training has been largely individual and small group exercises, but now we are to function as a cohesive unit, practising daily jumps from our Dakota aircraft. Here is a glorious place for training; all level fields and few trees, and the town's mellowed stones and tiled roofs and its mediaeval courtyards will bear witness to our presence long after we have gone! For, of course, the young ladies, as we must call them, have little choice now that their young men are away and intent on conquering the Nazis instead.

Officially, we are instructed not to keep written records, nor to identify street names, and road signs are all but obliterated. Then again we are denied the opportunity to despatch letters to the Crimea, or the Russian steppes or wherever else we have escaped, so that won't stop us. In any event, we have a reputation to maintain; we're 'nierecznosc' or *awkward customers* in Polish. Rules won't stop us! Our three years in this country have taught us that that remains the only way to deal with commanders who prefer that we die for Britain and not for our countrymen back home. How they cemented this deal, or who really is in charge, and how we gain respect, who the hell knows?

There's not much time now to wait, rumour tells, and though nerves are on edge, the numerous jumps and compass and weapons training should prove what we know already. That we are amongst the best. Deep in our bones, we hate those who have stolen our country and taken away family and friends, and that gives us the spirit to fight. The locals too have little difficulty in understanding this sentiment, and are forever congratulating us for it. They are even amazed that we might be capable of expressing this in their own language! But we share a similar view of life, don't we? Irreverent, humorous and cynical all at the same time, and take us out of uniform and sharing cigarettes and favourite drinking haunts, you couldn't even choose between us.

17

I'm spending more time at Rene's now, though she cautions I'm to blame for her falling behind with her studies. Her studies! Some nerve, eh? I spotted that three-cross motif on her university building the other day, and she tells me they are St Andrew's crosses. We noisily and childishly debate the merits or otherwise of *crucifixion orientation,* this way or that. Except neither go for the upside-down hanging of early Christianity! And then we get to Brueghels in Amsterdam, and a copy does exist here, painted by his son.

"What you're sayin' we look at some pictures?" playing up my Canadian. "Since we're already acquainted with the subject."

She feigns to consider my invitation, but then says. "So why not view something four-legged instead?" with more than a little of nuance to the question. A dig for sure, but I get it, Rene. My long-expired promise come to haunt me.

"The animals, remember? And there's no time like the present."

She waits. I consider, but now, "Come on. We go out" in that declamatory way that allows no scope for dissent. So Irene. So Dutch. She's taking no prisoners now, grabbing me and bundling her coat in one swift movement. Likewise, speedily Dutch. This is how they built on from their Golden Age.

Seeming like everyone else in this city, Rene only dresses in pneumatic outerwear, looking like nothing so much as one of the ranked assemblies of Michelin men, and she sure is in a hurry. Outside it's feet-stomping weather and after a little more than a few moments, the cold and vicious easterly tells that good sense says I should invest in a Michelin too. But, hey, isn't it just good to be out and about again? And now we two are together once more.

"Fancy a pancake?" I suggest as we set out, because I am quite helpless without a plan for the day that fills the gaps between meals, where my stomach demands satisfaction.

It's only a few streets away, I know, and yes, there is the cafe sign that's unmistakably *touristic* for a Dutch favourite, pancake being emblazoned across windows dripping with condensation. Also, an especially good look, for it's sure to be warm in here.

"So why not indulge, my returning hero?" she says as she steers me through the door and "Pancakes with everything," scrawled on the wall panel in that faux-authentic scrip.

We squeeze into a corner of tiny white decorative tiles decorated with kitch scenes of Amsterdam life, all in the standard Delft blue.

"Clearly, no problem for your language block," she scorns, scanning a slate-board with chalk offerings scribbled in English. She's merciless in her scoldings for me not having a single word of Dutch in all this time. Except for the apple cake and cream, of course.

We're not yet warm enough to dispense with coats and Rene says, "Why don't I choose and then you choose and then we'll swap around half way? Like the romantics we truly are."

So here I am envying the Irene line in wackiness as she debates her order. Not a local voice to be heard until the server arrives to scribble our plates order onto his pad. Hers the one to be generously strewn with bacon; this one to be seriously overloaded with Canada's favourite condiment.

And I reckon that this suited Irene's scheme all along, and you're quite right; this girl is truly massive.

18

There's been fog and drizzle around for almost two days now, and it doesn't seem as if it will ever clear. It also lends a sour cabbage-type smell to the fields about, and comes as a real reminder of home. A local here warned that the easterlies come all the way from Russia, right over the Urals, so I'm not altogether surprised by that sudden chill.

Now, though; a change. A complete break in the cloud, and I'm mulling my thoughts as I collect my parachute and kit. We traverse around the fleet of Dakotas and the sound of intermittent firing of props, the acrid smell of aircraft dope, and head towards the tarmac-coated and camouflaged briefing rooms, roofs painted to match the nearby fields.

A multitude of tongues echo around the place. Cossack, Russian and the pure Polish, mostly spoken by our officers, and above it all, cutting through the rest, the bombastic nasal bluster of our gum-chewing Yank friends, hailing from all points north, south, east and west, marshalling loading trollies, light weapons, and seeming chaos.

The briefing room is dank and low-lit, and blinds cover all window lights. There can't be more than a quarter of our strength here, I imagine. Other units are being briefed elsewhere to their particular specialisms: gunners, engineers, medics and military police.

We rise, somewhat haphazardly, at the arrival of our Commanding General, Sosabowski, but we know he has lived the life and has worked amongst us from the earliest days in Fife. He's a man who has the loyalty of every single one of us. Far from his first battle, this particular one. He has fought the Germans back home, survived capture and escape, and has gathered together his countrymen from France and a ragtag-and-bobtail collection of volunteers from who knows wherever. Most too have glimpsed him in the 'Monkey Grove', the purpose-built tower to simulate a drop. So, a fellow warrior amongst us and not just a man of rank.

The lights dim, the giant projector whirs into action, almost drowning out the softly spoken intelligence officer with his pointer. It's the map we expect, of course, what else? For we would be lunatics not to have put together in the last weeks the various and obvious clues. It has to be flat, patently, and close to the present Allied battle lines, which means Northern Belgium or Southern Holland. The rumour-mill has settled on the bridges at Nijmegen or Arnhem for a long while now. Both still held by the Germans, and now at last, here's Montgomery's favourite target confirmed.

Lots of technical info to follow (take-off estimated 1400 hours), and here comes the by-now routine, motivational spur.

"Never forget how it must feel to be under the heel of a hated enemy for so long," he parrots.

And, as one, on our feet and bitterly voicing what denied us the opportunity to help free our own countrymen and women alongside the uprising in Warsaw, a mere matter of weeks ago.

19

St Nicholas 1944

This will be a festive season that no one over there in the west of Holland will ever forget. For not a single glimpse of happiness or of joy: no Black Pete, no seasonal gifts, no firecrackers at New Year. Just for the absolute evil of the Nazis.

Now that we can safely listen to the radio, there is nothing any longer that can protect us from what we should not know. Yes, it's true that our queen and government have been safe in England, but now that Wilhelmina has made it absolutely clear that every Dutch man and woman in this country is on the Allies' side and for the unconditional return of all our rights, and because our railway workers have halted all trains in support, we are to be painfully starved to death. Nothing at all will be allowed up from the south, where vital harvested supplies are stored, and fuel and goods are produced.

What's more, an especially severe winter, with the canals and rivers frozen over, means no hope for relief from any other direction either. There are already beginning many reports of catastrophic shortages of everything, and no fuel to keep homes warm and for production to be maintained.

So now we know for certain, if we didn't always know it, that it isn't just we Jews who are the enemy, it's the whole of our nation to be punished. They say the shops are already empty over there, and, what little there is left, is guarded closely to limit everyone to the five hundred or so calories, the daily allowance: hardly sufficient to keep young and old alive.

People are stripping doors and ceiling trusses to burn on their fires. Children are scraping the remnants of margarine barrels, and yes, it's true, now the elderly are dying in their hundreds. Our hearts go out, even if we are lucky enough that, here in the south, there's the growing of early vegetables and still-stored grain around and about on our farms. And who doesn't keep rabbits and chickens in the countryside and away from the cities?

But what can be done for the rest, when our brave friends are still fighting and dying their way through Europe? And un-liberated Holland is a little stump behind German lines, surrounded by seas on one side, rivers on its flanks and the enemy before, locking all in?

20

We are eerily silent on our three-hour flight, and for far more than the usual tensions of sickness and fear. The original battle plan was first delayed, and now has changed, so that we are landing behind enemy lines to the south of the Rhine. Tell me; how do we now have any element of surprise, for if *we* understand precisely the logic of a pincer movement, then so too will the enemy. And, now approaching the jumping zone, why are many of our transports turning away and flying in another direction, to the west? But we are ordered to fulfil the battle plan, so we cross our fingers and we jump into the usual welcome of mortar and machine-gun fire.

Amazingly, it didn't take us long to assemble, the wind and piloting being kind. Nine hundred-plus men and equipment; a veritable miracle considering the myriad languages spoken. And for the first time, news that the ferry here at Diel intended to carry us across to relieve those trapped at Oosterbeek; that ferry is particularly ill-located at the bottom of the Rhine! And whilst the Brits have promised to supply rafts, and we have inflatable rubber boats, they also assured us that they would hold the bridge! And we are still targets!

We hear the radio traffic reporting wounded (the dead will have to wait till nightfall), so we must take up defensive positions and dig in for battalion commanders to gather to decide Plan B. Little now that can be done, other than launch our light mortars at likely sources of snipers and machine-gun nests.

As we wait for dusk, our new instructions are that we are to cross the river in the middle of the night. We have to do our best to relieve the besieged units and our headquarters close to the Arnhem Bridge.

21

He's still seriously preoccupied, my Tom. I can see it now. He says that he wants most of all to slow the pace, and to work out his next steps, and especially where he's going with this research. He worries, with all the current interest in social media, whether he might have seriously underplayed the influence of the then newly-developing technologies of newsreel, cinema and radio.

"They also help set a narrative, don't they, Rene, create heroes and villains? After all, if a population's listening and watching is largely directed from the centre…and with your mood music set, there's only one impediment remaining. You only have to control the positioning of the key chairs and who gets to sit in them. So, get to harness the opinion-makers, the directors and financiers, the spokesmen, editors and propagandists. Close down the opposition; the courts and universities. And now you have screened your placemen—"

"And women," I'm tempted to add, but can you imagine his agitation with all of this heavy thinking on top of Oma's health and a soon-to-be disappearing friend who always had his ear for his ideas?

He's not resolved his issues with maple syrup either! Why the hell can't he use the tissues like the way they're intended, rather than screwing them up into tiny balls and methodically prising them apart once more; sliver by sliver, as if unpicking his layers of unresolved history. And as for the question of today's planning.

"I'll give you one clue now, Tom. We're not quite there yet, obviously, but it involves living objects sometimes gifted with four legs, though not necessarily."

But here we go again, no relief either to be gained from my way with riddles.

"What is it with dictators and their animals, Rene? Don't they all love them? All those snaps of the moustachioed one, him and his mistress and his German shepherd, of course. Children and dictators alike. They all adore animals, don't they? Children, okay, dictators—"

"You're dodging my clue, Tom," I say, but he's on a roll.

"Must be something in it. Mussolini had his pet lion, Lenin has his cat and so on. Can I tell you a joke?"

"You can tell me anything you like, as long as—" lunging to grab him by the tabs of his jacket and half-wrestling him away from the table, and him protesting all the while.

"Hey, I'm being really serious here. Why did Lenin never ever name his cat? That's the question," struggling to his feet.

"I have no idea, Tom. Now put on your scarf."

"Okay. Check. You want the answer? Nobody really knows, Rene. For you can only name a thing when you own it, and, in a communist society—"

It all went badly wrong at the zoo.

22

By dawn, we're across the water. We've lost too many men I know, and now the river crossing itself is under fire, so no way back that way. And we've discovered that the Germans also hold the larger parts of this side of the bank.

I ask to use a set of field glasses, stand as tall as I might on the tips of my boots, and this Polish soldier glimpses the bridge for the very first time.

23

I've been storing up my words for three years or more. After all, they're the only things I've had to save, and, if such words really do exist in the universe, they are failing me now.

After the disasters way back at Arnhem and the failure to secure the bridge, the Nazis now are finally beaten, and naturally there is much rejoicing. But many of the Dutch have been starved and half-frozen, with little ones still scavenging on the streets and surviving from the remnants of food bins.

The Queen speaks graciously on the radio and tells that every single Nazi law is overturned and people can go back to how it was before. But for all our joy, I must stay realistic and know that perhaps even harder times lie ahead. The whole country is ruinous.

Forgive me if I appear ungrateful, for I know I am still here only because of others' bravery, whose risks were much greater than mine; a girl who can't even walk past the farmyard geese without quaking in my boots. So, whilst the waiting goes on, let me tell you, dear diary, of the secrets I've been hiding inside for so long.

Yes, I have my new family of the kindest people in the world; a young widowed mother—who has her own burden of grief and will never allow me to speak to it—and her two younger children, quite unlike a family I'd ever known before.

In the first few months, I needed to keep my head down because my Dutch didn't seem too convincing, except luckily, I had already picked up the Amsterdammer way of saying things. And anyone out there would recognise that. The mother would tell I'm so shy that 'my mouth is always buttoned up'.

So here I have spent most of each day with this 'distant aunt', helping out on the farm with the animals, and packing the unsaleable meat and bones to be loaded onto trucks and sent on to the zoo. What we receive in return, you could know for a kilometre at least!

I'm pleased my shelterer and friends are religious people. They truly believe in the goodness of everything and everyone around us, which has only been turned bad by sheer evil. So, they go to their church and they pray before meals, and we agree; as we are of the same God, why should some be a six-pointed star with 'Juden' embroidered and a large red J in our cards? And as time has gone by, my Dutch is likely as good as any native person's, and no one suspects anything. Or if they did, they were real patriots and didn't tell. Just as before in the kindergarten.

24

The entrance to Artis is rather grand with gold eagles atop the iron gateways. Everything green and black. Our instinct is to turn right past the shop and the *traffic* side at home, like here in Holland, but I'm up for a challenge today, disregarding the sign.

"Let's skip the planetarium, Rene, stick to the earthly beings," I suggest, as I steer her past little canals fronted by plant borders, though looking a tad neglected at this time of the year. Just stubby grass. But a gazelle feels confident enough to venture out of its shelter, and the birds are squawking busily in the trees as the few early insects begin to emerge. And the sun is doing its best to banish the worst of the chill.

"What's with the bullfrogs, Tom?" she says as we sweep a corner. Weirdly, we discover it's not the frogs but pelicans alongside the flamingos, daring to dry out their wings and squawking furiously. In any event, the reptile house is now looming, and strange coiled and creeping creatures exhibited within, the turtles riding each other bareback, inviting strictly non-reptilian thoughts! Not to be conveyed to Irene, of course, who is more concerned to ignore any knife and fork signs and is clearly headed in the direction of the elephants' enclosures.

"Do you know the guys who thought out this zoo had little time for locks, keys and iron bars, Tom? They were just way genius of their time. Brilliant formula, isn't it? You just need water to distance the most dangerous, and, for many of the rest, natural barriers like steep rocks and crags for ibex and other climbers. Hey presto. Magic."

Now it's beginning to drizzle steadily, and we can do with warming up.

"So, listen up you. No nonsense. We really should get to see the elephants first. They're *the* big attraction at present. New enclosures and all that."

The signage, as we arrive at the most northerly edge of the zoo looking directly out onto a canal, declares a bull recently added to the herd. However, elephants always look back to front to me: that trunk should surely be a tail? I ask Rene if God made a slip-up with the development plans. She declares aloud that if I cannot be serious about any damn thing—and no, we don't have elephants in Canada Rene, and—so it goes.

And, for me, I'm wondering just what would be the chances of getting across that canal back in wartime; searchlight-lit and patrolled as it would have been, even with the help of two little girls and their zoo map, and I am back in Oma territory once again; a place I'm warned I shouldn't really be, so I suggest, what say we do the lions next? I'm still fazed by the badly-designed elephants, clearly, but Irene is in lockstep.

"Just do your walking-on-ahead routine, Tom, and you can't miss."

As I consider myself more the 'lion man', I power straight down through a long tunnel ahead with its echoing waterfall rush, and turn left at the end signpost.

Rene's still out of sight, but nothing to be seen this way, except a large high savanna notice. What's with this confused signing anyway? Now, Rene emerges from behind me as I begin to retrace my steps.

"This is a real gong show. It's got to be the other way," irritated now and spotting another pointer for the reverse direction, and I'm on the receiving end of that *idiot* glance. "Two signs in opposite directions, Tom. What does that leave you?"

I'm sure baffled. And to be honest, not a little embarrassed too.

"Try up," she says.

"Up?" I puzzle.

"Didn't you catch the staircase sign in the tunnel. Stone steps pointing up?"

"I'm not a mind reader, Rene. Seems you're a million miles more observant than me."

"So maybe you're always too much in a hurry, Tom."

I feel like glued to this spot.

"So, are we going up?"

A niggling thought that she knows way too much about this zoo.

"It's almost like you've been here before, Rene. I mean, you seem pretty savvy around all the twists and turns."

Silence.

"So that was pitched as a question, Rene."

Still nothing from Rene.

"I mean, don't I get an answer?"

"Maybe just leave it there, Tom. Seems far more like an accusation from your side than a question. Just cool it, will you?"

Jeez. No way I'm any good at this kind of stuff—just stressing me out.

"Is it really any of your business anyway, Tom? What I do."

"Just a question of honesty, Rene, that's all. I guess a guy deserves it."

At that moment I want the ground to swallow me up, to start again at the beginning.

"Unbelievable, isn't it Tom? It's a zoo day. No more than that. And you, here, acting like a jilted lover. All high and mighty. I can do without this stuff, you know."

"So just answer me, will you?"

Jesus, Mary. I'm all tensed up, I know; too angry and too much of a coward to ask her the question just out straight. And no, I don't want to hear the answer anyways. My instinct says stay calm, but my head is confused, whirling massively, and my body tells me this can't be doing me any damn good and, then, the very last thing I need to hear.

"You don't own me, Tom. I've got a life."

She walks away, fumbling in her pockets, turns and throws me back my spare keys.

25

Dear Jaap,

I hadn't planned to write this letter, but, you know, events? I want to say straight-out you've been so thoughtful and concerned about Tom, and yes, he's a wonderful guy, but I'm not sure he's right for what I want at this moment in time. So yeah, we've had what you might say is a bit of a bust-up, but I guess that's not rare in couples, is it?

We're great in the bedroom department (am I allowed to boast that?), but it's these small, persistent hangups at the moment which seem to knock him right back. How's he gonna be with the bigger stuff?

Sure, I understand he's saying goodbye to a close friend, and his work's maybe not going as sweetly as intended, but I'm not certain I want to be his closest confidant when he's behaving so needy. And I haven't even come to his obsession with his Oma yet!

It's been going this way for a while now, Jaap. It's not a flash in the dark. And forgive me if I can be a little straight with you about the roots of it all. After all, we're all charmed by a stranger who, at the very beginning, is pretty much not like us in every which way, and then you can delight in unpacking the quirks and nuances and everything. And that's cool.

But honestly, I'm missing the sheer stress-free thing of the everyday familiarity of *joking native.* You know; that you get from people and places you know best. Like the ground rules you've always taken for granted. Weirdly, and this worries me, I'm not even sure our emotions run on the same trajectory. Sometimes, it all feels so locked in, I just have this deep urge to laugh out loud for a while and not be a solace for his family thing.

Please, take it from me, Jaap, this note's not meant as a farewell, and far from a plea for justification, but Tom will surely sound you out at some point, and I hope you appreciate my take on things. We two will cool it for a while and see how things work out.

I feel lucky that you and I have shared this connection, and I send Tom's Oma all the very best for her health. And maybe we'll get to hook up in person one day?

Love,
Irene.

26

5 May 1945

Though we are at some distance from our neighbours, it's Liberation Day, and everyone is invited to meet the 'real me'. Except, on my life journey, I seem to have misplaced that person I once was. The one, and now seeming a lifetime ago, who had a devoted friend who, even now, can never be put out of mind.

Everyone around is new family and new well-wishers, and the German nightmare and our pets and those left behind, now seems as little more than dread portend. And yes, 'a little teacher' always, even when helping at the kindergarten. But then gifted with a new family name that threatened to cut away like a knife from the one lodged in your past.

And I know that everyone here is buttoning up what they truly want to ask because my 'aunt' has already explained the traumas along the way, and my new 'little cousins' too young to understand anyway. And me with only one question left to answer: is there anything or anyone at all left back in that previous life?

The barn is strung with bunting and someone has brought a wind-up gramophone, but only one record, 'Blonde Mientje', about a resistance girl with a 'heart of barbed wire' which plays over and over. We have white asparagus from the nearby farm; asparagus with everything: in the soup, in omelettes and even a sweetened pie. I try out a speech in my head which I know isn't very good because what is there to say, other than "Thank you from the bottom of my heart, and how can I ever repay you?"

And then, tearing up for what I dread might await me after all this is over. Because not one of the 'when' questions gives up a single, certain answer.

27

I'm running some of my recent thoughts past my buddy Bart. Not quite the farewell I imagined, though. No partying here, no Irene, no Gunilla either. Is this female solidarity, I worry? And then, foolish me, for being so crazily paranoid.

Bart tells me he's relaxed that I'm much cooler now on my take on history, but let's face it, every new generation keeps puzzling away at it; it just shifts in direction and emphasis. And that has to be the hope, surely? If we can't reframe after stumbling over some unsuspecting stepping-stones, then take the time to look back carefully at the route chosen.

"Consider the vocabulary, Bart, the trademark signs and symbols through which like-minded nationalists connect. Fewer fancy uniforms in these times, admittedly, but yes, still the huge rallies (what is it with crowds?). And now, the newly-weaponised culture wars which serve the same purpose as bullets; to diminish, to instil fear or envy."

Bart happily rarely interrupts if it's our work that's at stake. He's cool to sit back. And then to pile into me later with his critique!

"Take the Hitler salute, for instance and the *Sieg Heil*. What's that really about? Surely innocent enough on the face of it? But in Germany in the 30s, children were taught to practise the salute from a young age and might even be reprimanded if failing to use it. Generally, a salute is an acknowledgement of another's superior rank, but in *Heil Hitler-ing*, think about it, you're going so much further, engaging as co-conspirator, as actor and as recipient. It's like you're allies in a collaborative project. Don't we all see the wave from a boatload of tourists? And don't we all wave back?

"Now take the requirement to display the Jewish star; pure genius, in that it distinguishes, but also marks as much the observer as it does the wearer. For sure, you first still need the guy with the massive megaphone to say, 'The nation is sacrosanct above the people'. But then add in, 'The Jew has swindled us. The Jew is corrupt', and now consider. Highlight the tropes of ugliness, wealth and filth, and even if this Jew is none of these things, the star proclaims it's a Jew. So, I'm wondering now, a mongrel maybe, mixed in with the likes of us, and then the whole nation is made culpable, for allowing these things to take place."

For the first time, I take a glance across at my buddy. Is he really up for this?

"The displaying of the star thus amplifies the caricature. And before you know it, Tom, all human attributes and differences are smoothed away in this one unified *Jew*, endlessly reinforced on hoardings, in speeches, in newsreels, in radio.

"You do get that you can be something of a ranter, Tom?" Bart observes. "Not a criticism, buddy, far from it, but you sometimes just don't know quite where to stop."

I feel somewhat knocked back on my heels. Am I really deserving of this? Jeez. I'm merely trying to sort this real gong show in my head with a guy I'm fond of. And dammit he's soon to be away, and I'm not yet done, when there's a knocking at the door and hey, it's Hanny with her son. She is clutching a giant bottle, which I take to be not exactly a celebration of me and my musings.

Embraces done with, "A special drink on you, Bart? Why not? Don't suppose you have the necessaries?"

Bart squeezes past me into his pint-size kitchen, muttering along the way,

"And something soft for Harvey?" this child-man who has already presented to the whole world that he's reading the most recent authority on Spinoza. I joke to Hanny did she ever considered naming him Baruch, after his hero, when Harvey ambushes me with, "How's Rene?" I haven't even got that he knows the name, so careful have I been to keep stuff of the heart away from him, and I wonder if 'you know' is sufficient to help hold him at bay, even if it's not any more than I know. That *mum* look from Hanny appears to settle it.

"Everything already packed, Hanny, but no slog," as Bart emerges with a collection of Queen's Day tat of plastic, empty glass jars, can-opener, beers and the fizz. I offer Hanny the sofa as Harvey sprawls into the middle space, and I attempt a look as cool as it's possible when this young dude knows damn well I've been dumped.

And then Bart's fiddling with his phone as Hanny expertly twists off the foil and eases out the cork and Gunilla appears with a friend in minutes, as if by magic, and clutching a bottle for Harvey too. And now Hanny is telling of a new Holocaust Museum coming to Amsterdam soon, whilst I fret away that there is just that one person absent to make it the most perfect of farewells together.

28

The mobile buzzes, and a sure skip of a heartbeat, but I don't recognise the sender's number.

And then…—What if it's back home, and there'd be only one reason? Take a minute, calm down, dude.

Then I hear "Hey, buddy. How's things?"

That's no way doom, is it, so I reply with the usual: "Hanging, Jaap. Just hanging. What's news?"

"Thought I'd WhatsApp," he replies, and I want to tell him, no way I'm impressed. Streetwise just doesn't sit too well with a guy in his 70s. And that's not WhatsApp he's using.

"It's all your sister's hassling, Tom. Her deal. She's been over regular since Oma's illness. So, she's preaching Insta or Snapchat, or whatever the hell they call these things these days. And she gave me a heads-up. Anyway, knew you'd be pleased."

"Sure, why not, Jaap, and you can keep me up to speed with Oma at the same time. So, shoot away, how is the old girl?"

"Happily sticking in there, and sticking it to us likewise. Same old story, same old Freyja."

"Weird though," I offer. "All this thinking doom and gloom, but we'll all miss her when she's gone, right? And a big gap for you to fill too, eh, Jaap? Just how will you doodle through the days?"

"Never give it a second, buddy. No worries. Maybe I'll take up reading like you."

"Hey, that's just mean, man. You get it's the *after-the-reading* sorts the men from the rest? And next, then you'll need to learn writin'," giving it out now like we're two old boys.

"So, how's that going, Tom. The writing I mean?"

Now I guess exactly where this is headed.

"The writing?"

"Hey. Not that we're concerned, buddy, but no news is…And when we first—"

"Got yer, Jaap. Just stop there. Quit reading my mind, will you?"

An awkward silence.

"Jeez, you're not wrong, though. So damn right. Someone's got to keep an eye out on me. I say not so grounded at present, Jaap, to be straight. Things and that."

"You okay for dollars…I mean if it's—"

"Fine, Jaap. Just fine. I promise I'll touch base when I'm down to my last bowl of poutine."

"Next time around, I'll have Oma on," he adds.

"Just tell her I'm well, will you, Jaap? I'm well."

Curious that there's no mention of Irene, though.

29

Summer 1945

Not a single word back from my enquiries. I know things are in chaos everywhere, and maybe letters aren't even being delivered to their destinations, but it is breaking my heart. And then I know that people worry about me too, for my safety and whereabouts, which is some kind of consolation. And, back in my head once more to Freyja, Mutti and Papi, and the cousins, and so it goes.

There's more than ever to do on the farm, of course, for feed and fertiliser are still in short supply, even with all the Americans' assistance, and that really helps concentrate the mind. But it's now, in the relative calm, I can try and puzzle out what they did to us and why. And; can you see? It's not so complicated after all.

It's pretty-much a straightforward game plan. Firstly, they strip you of your rights as citizens, and, always hoping for the best, you hold your breath. For after all, you are still alive. But then they directly attack your entire being by defining you as a person only by your religion. So now, you're beginning to weary and gasp for air. Still alive, true, but now less than human. After that, only one last thing remaining to you: how best to escape, to get away; how to cancel your grandparents. Take the stone from off the grave. Understandably, denying your Jewishness isn't easy, even the scientific experts fail. But why not try, for divorce or sterilisation are murderous to the body and soul, are they not? And at the very last, and at that moment you give away your child, then you're no better than a dead person walking.

Maybe I am the luckiest girl alive after all; having hidden here miles away from anything, and hardly a Nazi uniform in sight, whilst the stealers, and forgers of my documents were living daily with their fears? This way and that, so my thinking goes. You can't really see it, and sometimes I resort to inventing a whole day in my head that's just like the movies we used to watch together at the Tuschinski Theatre, and later we're gathered around our table or Freyja's or the aunts and the uncles, and faces swim once more into clear focus, and the stories we tell, and the future we plan, making everything bearable grow ever more sweet.

30

A letter from Oma. No surprise there. She and Jaap have been putting their heads together for sure, and are out to rescue me! Same old roundabouts: do I have enough in way of dollars, am I keeping warm, do I have a toque, how's the work going?

It may appear grudging, but how different from hanging with your folks when you want to flee the nest, right? The old girl has even told me to '*git'r done',* as *she* once did, to button down with her own studies all those years ago! So okay, she's in her nineties, and I'll forgive the intrusion.

But how much of this is Grandma, and how much is Jaap? And the rest of the family? Yes, I may be in s…creek, but leave me alone, won't you? I've too much thinking time now, and that's a bumma, and I'm stuck with too few answers as to what's next.

And I cannot get Irene out of my mind. Or rather, me with Irene. Wasn't it all over a simple trust thing, I mean? Shouldn't she be straight with me, of all people? Or am I just another insecure sucker who doesn't count tops in her eyes?

Maybe Hanny could help here. But how do you even begin to steer a path in that direction?

"Hanny, a word. On the girl-boy thing—"

Let it lie, why don't you? Plenty more fish in the sea. But then I'll have to come clean with Jaap about a girl, and that's a pride thing.

31

Royal Artis Zoo, Amsterdam
21 June 1945

Dearest Eleonore,

We want you to know that we haven't forgotten you here. Yesterday we had a Board meeting. The Director has sent his best wishes and apologises for the delay in replying, but you will understand that a zoo, like any human, doesn't easily recover from trauma.

We have had to undergo a complete inventory here, for poor feeding and too few keepers and other staff means a dilution of our animal stock. That sounds ruthless, doesn't it, because you know the animals are our friends, but sometimes one has to be cruel to be kind. Little by little too, our best men are returning from labour in Germany. And at the same time, our younger female keepers can make plans for their futures, perhaps to marry and have families of their own.

Our human 'guests' are finally liberated, you'll be pleased to know, and we are putting back the bricks and mortar and mosaics of the records office. You probably went 'up in flames' in the inferno there! After the bombings, there was general chaos, of course, but the greater good was that many records were erased and the Nazis found it much harder to check the authenticity of people's papers.

Now, to come down to earth. We would very much like you to visit us here as soon as you are able, because we have something special for you that you should best receive face to face. And now we can say that most of the news is good news. Perhaps about Freyja too? We haven't seen her here for a while.

We remember that you girls were the very best of friends, and that must have made things difficult. But let's look on the bright side. We have a new arrival here at the zoo, a visitor from London, as a mark of friendship between our two countries. She will be a quite a surprise when you visit. We have given her a special name. But don't let on to Mr Sunier!

Your friend,
Gert.

32

Hey, you both. What say I lay my cards on the table and come straight out clean. Irene and I are no longer an item. There. That's done. You wouldn't expect an explanation, I hope. These things just come to pass. And *you'll* get what I'm saying for sure, Jaap.

Means I can spend much more time doing what I'm here for and maybe widening my circle of buddies. Also, I get that I should be much more involved in local affairs. That's my thinking now. I'm not registered to cast a vote here, but, get this; the whole country seems like it's losing direction. Just like once upon a time, eh Oma? The racial purity stuff, the great replacement theory, too many Muslims, language and culture, men and women, you name it. No one can get it together. I'm told one of the great gifts of the Dutch project from the earliest times, for co-operation, for differing opinions and remedies and so on, has always been 'out there' (even if ironically). But what happens when some are shouting far too loudly, or escalating through social media, or not even paying attention anymore? What then?

And it's not just the centuries gone either, though maybe we Canucks do need reminding of it. Right here on the streets of Amsterdam, the assassinations of provocateurs like Forteyn and Leo van Gogh. Shouldn't that scare the pants off us?

'Nuff said. Back to you in Montreal now. How's the hospital routine going, Oma? I know the struggles of veins and ligatures and needles in and out drives you bats, but I gather you've something more permanent now? And Jaap is doing his bit too? And no fear either he's doing the business to my end, keeping me in the frame, and he promises we'll do a real face-to-face hook-up in the next days. Quite the professional now is Jaap with his *Insta* and his *WhatsApp!*

Now, those rumours I've heard of a brand-new museum commemorating those grim times of deportations and the holocaust look set to become a reality, so we'll keep a keen eye open here. I guess there'll be a few survivors still? Who knows?

Missing my old buddy, Bart, sad to say, and haven't seen the swastika guy for yonks. S'pose we're all moving in different universes now. Shouts about the Liberation Day coming up. The Dutch do it real big here, so I'll watch out for the ghost of our family soldier hero!

Much love to you guys,

Tom.

33

Late Summer 1945

I'm remembering a girl so desperate to write, but was denied paper and pen for her own and others' safety. And she wanted so much that her friend would know that she was still safe. That friend was still so special to her that she invented a thought letter, believing once more—as she did as a child—in magic. It felt like her last act of love, and now, less than two years later, that same girl gazes at the building where, for a time, she was a 'little mother' to countless sorrowful children, all the while their parents were confined in a theatre prison just across the street, a place that had once brought equal parts joy and excitement to the good people of Amsterdam.

Not much has changed since then. Surprisingly, the girl was only a little older than the children she cared for. Yet, she was entrusted with the wisdom of Solomon to maintain the bicycles and keep the children calm. Why not? For everyone in Holland once had bicycles, except not everyone to carry infants wrapped tightly and hidden inside panniers for an escape to freedom. And at the very same time, to be tasked to keep watch on the trams passing by, and to wish for them to halt for passengers, even if only for seconds, in order to provide cover for the hasty exit of carriers through the front doors.

And that same girl, taking a different route daily to her temporary place of safety in a small attic in a Royal Zoo famous for treating its inmates, not as curiosities, or even as dangerous, but as part of the same universe we all inhabit and share.

And, still and forever, asking the same question over and over. How does a mother or father, aunt or uncle, truly bear to offer a child to a complete stranger, trusting only in common humanity and knowing that might be the very last moment they will ever be together? And consider this also. Give me any reason on earth why a fellow human being would wish to force such a choice between a single slim hope of survival and a certain death?

34

Tom buddy.

Some things just have to go in letters! You're a darned idiot, Tom. No, just joking, but with this talk you've set Oma on another of her Eleonore binges. She's even convinced she could get to you in Amsterdam! A joke, eh, given she's finding it impossible now even to scribble her own name in greetings cards and letters.

We'll be arrowing down the Power of Attorney route before we know it. She can't so much as hold a pen, let alone a passport! Anyway, the deal is that she relays what she'd like you to know, and I am authorised to pass it on. No change there then!

Her memory is still a conundrum though. Nothing around for an age, and then out of the blue, she reminds me that she had promised she'd fill you in a little more about her times back then. Before it's too late!

Anyways, she dives down the route that the Dutch have forever suffered from this acute malaise, where they unashamedly tailor their long-held principles precisely when it suits. She was telling that when the Canadians first arrived as liberators, they were the acclaimed heroes of the hour. But, before you know it, it soon soured. You bet it did. These guys were, oh so more easy-going than the natives and, you know, young men being young men and that; alcohol and girls, the old Calvinist instincts come piling back on. I'm scribbling this down as I remember her telling.

So anyway, your great grandpa would walk her home, and sure, they may have kissed and embraced on the doorstep (and, of course, there had to be more!). But then, whose business was it anyway? No twitching curtains in Holland, they boast, and yet much peering through plate glass doors and windows for sure, says Oma. And then the duty a parent has towards a child? A child in need of support and advice. And was there any deal more when her best friend disappears?

And so it goes, Tom. The sins of the fathers! And mothers. Who knows? For me, all is just a blank; I don't recall a single word of all this growing up. I guess with her shame and locked-down an' all, it just never got talked about. And when I mentioned the news of you and Irene, you know what she said?

"That's just what they did to me. Stole the best thing in my life."

Jaap, with affection.

35

Autumn 1945

I've lived this day in my head for many hundreds of hours. The day of my first return to a once-happy life to discover if anything at all remains of all that was dearly loved. Of course, I have had few hopes of what might have become of our home, for letters returned to sender tell their own story, don't they? The Red Cross too say they have no information, and what if the only news were to be life-destroying?

You wouldn't even call it a home if you were to be standing here alongside me now. Nor even a place of the most desperate refuge. Window frames and doors of the larger building all gone to fuel a thousand fires in the dread starvation winter. And everything now boarded and bricked up, the neighbours' houses too. And how, if at all, do you count the loss of loved and treasured possessions and everything that links us back to happier times and a family thread that is merely paused when relocating, or through loss? Lives once lived here that are now truly extinguished.

The zoo is expecting me at noon, and in this little time, I just need to stand and stare once again at that magic portal where, two years ago, the 'Alice tale' was pitched into reverse, and the hero students next door would pedal like dervishes to deliver their precious cargo to good and brave people all around Holland. And all I see is nothing has changed much, for all around is still drab and uncared-for, which is not at all the Dutch way.

There are few people here now to bear witness to the miracles done within. Nor, any longer, a Dutch policeman at the barricaded doors of the Hollande Schouwburg to aid in the betrayal of all that is good and decent. But neither must we ever forget, not so very long ago, within that same building, people far braver than you and I who risked everything to expertly and dangerously delete the names of little lives from those lists that were no more than a death sentence.

And I wonder most of all, just what will come next? What is to follow? Who will be the deniers, the apologists, the plain 'just getting on with lifers'? And when, if ever, will justice truly be served?

36

I won't bother Hanny, immersed as she still is in those distant times. Photos, diaries, drawings, posters, pamphlets, underground and resistance literature. Paraphernalia all to be addressed, sorted, and translated, and think how lucky to have a willing buddy. So instead, I message Bart and Gunilla, who appear to have joined a travelling circus of assorted dreamers, dropouts and plain despairers in their mission to conquer every single part of the world except their own. 'In and around Greece at present', and they're okay they insist, which is surely more than I am, right?

Still, more than ever, I am missing you know who, and not a single instinct as to what to do about it. Tried working twice as hard, and jeez, no solace. Even considered joining the socialists, but they're way more focused on the future utopia than the here and now!

Tried Jaap, but he's the expert on splitting-up, isn't he? And as for the folks, pathetic too. Jeez, and then, hesitant to admit this, even considered Jos in the likelihood of a helpful intervention. Which shows just how damn crazy I'm becoming.

Desperate even. Spend too much time in the refectory, living in hope. The single coffee I can eke out, before the dark frowns of the servers say that I'm not aiding their best business interests, and it's now time now to go.

Wander the streets. Stare at the canal. Decide that Liberation Day hardly did it for me, if you get my pun. Running out of steam, running out of cash. Running out of time.

37

I really wish it to be the same old me as I turn the corner from the theatre and spot those familiar gates and the golden eagles atop, and the curious sentry-like box for admissions. Arriving here in the past, more often than not, a surge of hope. So please God, not to be pricked by disappointment or despair today. But joy! Standing by the entrance, a reception committee and the best-loved faces of *my* zoo; the Director, Mr Sunier and his lady secretary, who always made me hot chocolate, Gert the keeper, and a man who will 'show you your gift' they tell me. Now I see others in attendance who kept me safe when I most needed it.

Of course, the Nazis also truly loved this zoo, but they were always swamped by the teeming hordes of visitors still, as if a war truly wasn't happening, or was nowhere near to be seen. I recall I was never afraid at those moments. Perhaps only sometimes in the nighttime. Even so, unlike others, I was pleased not to be sharing my space with the 'native population', sometimes pacing, pawing and clawing at an iron divide mere centimetres away.

There are handclaps and kisses all around, and I'm embarrassed not to be offering dry cheeks, whilst, over and over, the same loving: "It's all right now, Eleonore. You're safe. Be calm." And their stroking my hair as if I'm a child. Then the images of Mumie and Papi, Freyja and uncles, aunts and cousins, all crowding out my brain and the leap and fall of this heartbeat near to desperation. And in the end, it is dear Gert who comes to the rescue, and with his embrace, he whispers an invitation, "The director wishes to speak with you later, if he may." As is his habit, he takes me by the hand, squeezes it hard and says, "No fear now" as he steers me away.

38

All is not bleak. There are lists posted at the Central Station of recent returners, whether from the camps or from Westerbork or goodness knows where else, and the locations where they can be newly registered.

The Jewish Coordination Committee is actively utilising American generosity to offer temporary shelter for the countless individuals who are presently in dire need. Friendly shopkeepers are offering window space for hastily scribbled and heart-breaking appeals for information about the missing. The Portuguese-Israelite Hospital, just around the corner from the theatre and zoo, has been hastily repurposed and now, now there is a House of Repatriation to help in planning futures for the displaced. And who knows, the Synagogue Ambulance Brigade may even chance upon Eleonore's family menorah in their efforts to retrieve Jewish treasures lost and stolen!

But consider also the wider population of Amsterdam, which too, has suffered terrible privations, and tell me; who should take the priority these days, and who should say what belongs to whom anymore and who decides? Who decides who are the guilty, and who is innocent and what retribution is to be handed out?

These present times are little less certain than before, and though the fabric of this beautiful city itself has suffered little harm, it will be many decades before the people's souls are truly healed.

39

"Please call me Mr Armand, Eleonore, as before. Nothing formal is required here, and nothing must change for us now, for we are all still family in spite of everything that has come between us." And, to humour me, he adds, "So sorry about your favourite chocolate drink. It's cocoa now for each and all of us. And not just for today either."

It's taken a while to try to calm my growing despair, and the fading light, glimpsed through the windows, fast slipping away beneath the horizon, only serves to mirror my present gloom. But the pure joy I feel when I now discover that mumie has been heard from—yes, it's true!! Can you believe? And my heart is exploding with an overwhelming surge of gratitude which can't be measured, no, not even in a lifetime. Nothing else matters, now; even a mention of my best friend's name would be as if I were punishing the man who has risked everything to plot my path away from danger. And what more has he risked by making his zoo a place of refuge? I should be weeping now rather for his bravery and for those who placed their trust in him.

And then it's the same old Mr Armand saying "But don't despair, my child, and always keep up your hopes, for without hope, what else is there? And I truly believe this country is building back its hope."

We sit in long time in silence now, until he rises to light the fast-darkening room. He telephones.

"We're all cheering up now, Gert, so perhaps you'd join us?"

It's at this moment I know I must steel myself to try my very best, for isn't that what mumie and papi would expect, and how can I let them down now? Mr Armand comes and sits alongside me on the sofa, and he quite surprises me by asking what I understand about my name. I can't once before ever recall wondering about it, and though, of course, he knows the naming secret I share with Freyja's father, it's clearly not that he's enquiring about.

"Understand, Eleonore, many parents worry themselves sick when it comes to naming their child. And I still remember arguing with Mrs Sunier over our firstborn. What if they were to turn out just like that least favourite neighbour? What if a rhyme or connection or some such invites ridicule or scorn; not intended of course, but there you are. You just have to live with it. Think how many of your German kindergarten friends will name their boys *Adolf* after these horrors gone by! Do you see what I'm getting at?"

I don't quite follow his direction, but that doesn't halt his flow.

"This is just one of our many reasons, Eleonore, that we refuse to give our animals pet names here. Too human a connection, you see. Too removed from their natural world."

And whilst Mr Sunier is busy playing the philosopher, I'm playing the detective game once more, and wondering where on earth this really is leading.

"Did you know that your name has a Hebrew meaning, child? Perhaps that was a consideration? For your parents, you understand."

I'm surprised by this, for we are not especially observant.

"You understand, Eleonore, that we're a scientific institute. The single purpose of our zoo, of course. Not all would agree, but there." Mr Armand often bookends weighty observations such as this, and always with the *but there,* which tells that the matter is settled and it doesn't brook of contradiction.

"So, we helped ourselves and did some thorough research as all good scientists, and learned that, in Hebrew, the *el* part in your name refers to God and the *or* signals light. And so, what a choice we have! We may decide one or the other, or even both together! And I can say, Eleonore, without contradiction, that since your very first coming to us here in the zoo, you've brought so much brightness into our lives that if there really is a God, he must deliberately have planned it. So much light, Eleonore," he says, placing his hand on my head, and though his is a head just full of science, he doesn't know a single thing about my emotions.

I feel wobbly once more, and I'm praying for a calming miracle when there's a tinkling of the bell.

"Visitors are expected" announces an assistant and, here is my Gert once more and yet another embrace, of course.

He sits at the grand table as if he is the boss, and the two of them pour a glass of something *quite strong,* as Papi would say, and a lemonade for me.

"Research now, Gert, do tell us about your research."

Apparently puzzled, but now roundly prompted, Gert tells confidently.

"Well then, Eleonore. Taking your name, we have discovered you have a very direct connection to the cat world. Of course, you would expect we keepers to know these things. True, Mr Director?"

I'm not sure what his silence suggests, but he goes on," And so, we are going to make just this one very special exception to our director's golden rule."

"The zoo's golden rule," smiles Mr Sunier, at which the door is pushed open, and there, cradling a bundle in his arms, is the keeper I first spotted at the gates. And this bundle is quite the most beautiful bundle of fur you might ever see.

"Come and join us, Lars," says Gert, "and bring along your gift."

He gently places the broad white paws of the bundle on my lap, and a long tail curls itself up around its ears as if to fit the space more exactly, no bigger than a baby.

"It's a snow leopard, Eleonore, but, for us, we prefer *panther auncia,* and our very first for us here at Artis."

And I can't resist the urge to stroke and caress, so little different it is from those recent days in the kindergarten. And unlike my human babies, this little one's a snowy white, and its back and tail are covered with the markings of tiny rosettes. But when she leans in to me for comfort just the same, and Lars says, "And everyone working at our zoo, from today will call her Eleonore", my heart truly breaks. "Every single one of us, and that even includes Mr Director here."

I'm unsure how I will be able to hold it all together, when Mr Armand saves me from myself. "And sentiment apart. I will insist on this. Absolutely no *Eleonore* to be inscribed on her living quarters."

He gets to his feet and turns to leave, offering as an afterthought, "As the great Mr Shakespeare himself observes,' That which we call a rose, by any other name would smell as sweet'."

He leaves us quite alone now, bemused, with the most perfect gift, and nothing much more than a parting shake of his head.

40

School of Postgraduate Studies.
Department of History.
University of Amsterdam.

Autumn term 2022

My dear Dean,

It is with great regret that I have taken the decision to step away from my immediate studies. I have benefited enormously from ready access to essential material both here, at the university, and elsewhere.

I would also like to commend to you the work of my research assistant, Ms Hanny Buhler, who has worked unstintingly, and now knows the subject ground without equal. Also, to my supervisor, who never failed me with sources, and only occasionally with direction!

My difficulties, you will see, have been in determining the appropriate focus of the work, and given some of the developments in recent politics in the Netherlands, that of the significance of this particular history of itself. Whether it aids *wiping the slate*.

I guess you do not find hesitancy over direction all that rare amongst those of us working at an advanced level, and I trust you understand my position. All will not be lost, however.

One possibility is a comparative study of the nationalist movements nearer to home in the Northern Americas, with those of Central Europe which emerged between the two 20th-century wars.

As for my present and future situations, I intend to return home to Canada, where, amongst other considerations, I have a close elderly relative who is not at all well. I have friends also in Quebec, where I was recently interested to discover that, as early as 1934, the National Christian Socialist Party was instituted.

I wish you with your students all the very best in your joint pursuit of learning, and I will happily and highly recommend your university to any prospective students you may wish to signpost my way.

PS: Forwarding address to follow.

Yours collegiately,

Thomas Murphy

41

Here I am surrounded by people whom I must learn to trust if I am even to begin to make plans for the future. In this place of shelter, returned from the camps, from hiding, from sheer accidents of fate, are gathered orthodox, liberal, sceptic and downright disbelievers. And few stories shared as yet. But no forgetting either, and long periods of silence, and an atmosphere of defeat, even in the face of victory. And on this particular day, perhaps more than any other of late, much of my future happiness will hang. For here I am, gifting back a family name to return it to the saintly man who first was born to it. And the dread thought that he may have forfeited too much in so doing.

In these recent years, I've come to understand him not just as the father of my dearest friend—almost as intimately as my own father, whose memory is now slipping away—but also as the hero whom Freyja could never be allowed to know about. This man, whom I can recognise even from a glimpse of the back of his head, the way he chews his food, the house he lives in, right down to the colour of my bedroom sink. This man who gifted me a sister—

He always warned the deceit would not hold under intense scrutiny, but Freyja's father truly does have a widowed, much younger cousin in the south. Why wouldn't she need extra help with her small children? And with the Jewish records in the city lying charred and burned by the resisters, making it impossible to decipher with the overgenerous dousing with the firemen's hoses. He was a powerful civil servant after all, who 'dealt with lots of important papers', Freyja would boast.

And now perhaps you can tell me; how is it ever possible to return back such heroism, if you are feeling small, slight and ungrateful in every moment since your return. For I owe seemingly the whole world a ticket for my life, and there are thousands upon thousands more just like me and lacking the words, if language this monumental truly does exist in the universe.

I see not much has changed in this place I once knew so well. Strewn around with mountains of sand and deep trenches, there are clear signals everywhere that the Nazis got in the way of the bedding-in process. My knocks on the door are not answered, and so there is nothing for it but to walk the length of the brown-brick street and around to the rear. There are some children playing hoop and stick and waving to me, but probably too young to know of Freyja. So I count the houses one by one from the corner number clearly marked, and I hope against hope. And yes, there I see it now; much more recognisable from the rear.

I stand and stare for a while, but the lower windows cast dark shadows that obscure everything within, and nothing else is visible. I'm tempted to give it all up when a door is thrown open.

"Can I help you, liefste?"

She's at a distance, but she walks towards the small gate, and before I can pluck up courage, she says, "I do hope you aren't searching for the previous occupants? They're long gone. The way they do, you know. Like lots others."

I want to understand if she has learned what has become of them, but however I persist, there's nothing she can help with, kind though she tries to be. As I thank her, and she wishes me luck, there is one last throwaway remark.

"I believe they left under a cloud, that's really all I know."

Perhaps that should act as a cautionary tale, but you know me; I'm not the one to give up. So I return to the front of the building, this time trying the bell of the nearest neighbours' house. It gives out a tinkling sound, and this time, some movement. Lace curtains are bundled aside, and I offer what I hope is an encouraging wave. A slow march to the door, and here's my story ready and hopefully convincing, because why else would I have known so much about this family? The gentleman answering, though courteous, seems to be holding something back. Yes, he knows when they left, not so long ago, and the size and markings of the removal van, and the weather that day and the talk…

"And the talk?"

He digs in at that. "My wife wouldn't thank me, and I shouldn't be gossiping to a stranger."

Still, I insist, "But they did everything for me. I have to thank them from the bottom of my heart."

He hesitates.

"You have to believe they truly saved my life."

And then, from within comes a voice, "Just send her away. Ger. She has no right to bother us."

My instinct tells I'm sure the gentleman is doing his very best, and just how many doors will I need to knock to get the answers I need; just how many removals companies to enquire?

So I ask instead, "I don't suppose you know where they went?"

Silence and a shrug of the shoulders, but, through the half-open door, "She got just what she deserved. What do you expect when you sleep around with soldiers?"

42

You do know you can never keep a secret from me, young Tom—never could! I'm disappointed, of course, but it's your life to lead, and who is this frail old lady to advise? After all, I made enough of my own mistakes along the way. And the curse of the historian too! You have to read life backwards when everyone is busy living it forwards. Back down the rabbit hole, so to speak.

And in the theatre of life, though everyone has a role to play, it is your task to discover the lead actors, the players of the bit parts and the hows and the whys.

And never forget this, my darling. Something Eleonore taught me so long long ago.

There are many, never forget, who will be written out of the script entirely, or will forever remain hidden in the wings. Lost to the accidental burden of belief.

Afterword

My two main characters, Eleonore and Freyja and their relatives, are wholly invented for my first book (*'The Why Question.'* Austin Macauley 2023) and are based around the characters of their two English namesakes, my own grandchildren. Almost everything else, except their stories, is set in an authenticated historical context.

Natura Artis Magistra ('Nature is the teacher of art'), now known as Artis Zoo, was first located in the leafy Plantage neighbourhood of Amsterdam in 1838. Its founders sought to promote *the knowledge of natural history in a pleasing and appealing way.* In addition to a zoo, it also contains a planetarium, an arboretum, a micropia and the Groote Museum. A part of the art collection is on display in the aquarium building of the zoo. During the time of the German occupation, the zoo became the hiding place for 250 to 300 men and women, escaping either arrest, forced labour or death. They included communists, resistance fighters and Jews. The Zoo's director really was Mr. Sunier, whom the children called Mr Armand, his Christian name. Mr Rudolf Polak was the founder and manager of the insectarium.

In an attempt to destroy the personal details of the population of Amsterdam, on 27 March 1943, fires were set in the municipal registry located in the zoo, which contained the names of 70,000 Jews. Despite their efforts, the resistors were able only to destroy around 15% of the documents. All were subsequently discovered or betrayed and executed.

The system of the Jewish Councils in Europe was set up by the Germans to require the Jews to contribute to the successful completion of the Final Solution. They were given responsibilities but no real power. They could only influence the way the lists of those to be deported were drawn up. For the rest, they merely passed on the orders of the occupiers. The last Jews were deported from Amsterdam in September 1943 when virtually all members of the Jewish Council in Amsterdam, too, were transported to Westerbork and the killing camps beyond. By comparison, the Jewish Council in Enschede, after the first razzias, urged Jews to go into hiding, a third of whom survived the war.

Carston is an invented name, but his real-life boss at the Expositor Office, Edwin Sluzker, remained in Westerbork for the duration of the war, continuing to play a vital diplomatic role throughout that time. His wife, Thea, acted as his secretary and survived alongside him.

Ferdinand Aus Der Funten, the Nazi chief in Amsterdam was initially sentenced to death after the war. The sentence was commuted in January 1951 to life imprisonment in the Koepel Prison in Breda. In 1989, he was one of the two remaining German war criminals in the Netherlands who were finally released, and he died three months later from a stroke. Hans Albin Rauter, the highest representative of the SS in the Netherlands, was executed in 1949.

The First Polish Independent Parachute Brigade was formed in Scotland on 23 September 1941. They received parachute and specialised training but did not enter combat until September 1944 as part of the attempt to capture the strategic bridge over the Rhine at Arnhem, which would have given the Allies a speedy back door into Germany and towards Berlin. Sadly, they did not succeed.

A number, including their Commanding Officer, were stationed in Stamford in Lincolnshire, the writer's home town for many years. It wasn't until May 1945 that the whole of the Netherlands was liberated. In the event, and during the previous winter, twenty thousand Dutch people died, and four and a half million were starved.

In total, during the four years of occupation, one hundred and seven thousand Jews were taken away from the Netherlands by the Germans. Initially, the Jews of Amsterdam were imprisoned in a theatre, *The Hollandsche Schouwburg*, and then moved to the Westerbork camp in the North of Holland, prior to deportation. Of all the Jews in the Netherlands, only five thousand and two hundred were to return. During that time, between five hundred and eight hundred infants and children were smuggled out to safekeeping. Many of these survived the war.

Pim Fortuyn, a Dutch right-wing politician, was shot dead in 2004 by an environmentalist and animal rights activist, nine days before the election. At that time, Fortuyn was leading the electoral race. His murderer claimed the politician had exploited Muslims as scapegoats and had *targeted the weak members of society*.

The Dutch filmmaker Theo van Gogh was murdered by Mohammed Bouyer in the same year, who had objected to van Gogh's representation of Ayaan Hirsi Ali's critical views of the treatment of women in Islam.

Geert Wilders, an anti-Islamist populist MP, won a dramatic victory in the 2023 Dutch general election by taking the largest number of seats of any single political party.